/ J

WITHDRAWN

D1521391

PEACEMAKER
PRIZEFIGHT

PEACEMAKER PRIZEFIGHT

•

Clifford Blair

AVALON BOOKS
NEW YORK

PRINTED IN THE UNITED STATES OF AMERICA
ON ACID-FREE PAPER
BY HADDON CRAFTSMEN, BLOOMSBURG, PENNSYLVANIA

To Master Man Suk Kim,
Sabom and friend,
who has motivated and inspired me in the martial arts.
Many thanks.

Prologue

In the ring the swarthy fighter hunched his heavy shoulders and bulled inside his opponent's guard. Right and left, right and left he began arcing vicious blows with his bare fists to the body of his taller foe. The motley crowd rumbled like a wild beast sensing a kill.

"James, this is cruel and barbaric!" Prudence Mc-Kay declared as if delivering a closing argument in the courtroom. Her tone penetrated the noise of the mob. "I want to leave immediately!"

Stark didn't take his eyes off the fighters. He squinted to see better through the haze of dust and tobacco smoke clouding the air inside the barn. "You're the one who wanted to get your client off the hook," he reminded loudly enough to be heard. "That's why we're here!"

"My services do not include attending a spectacle like this! I will not be subjected to—"

Up inside the ropes the taller man caved in under the battering he was taking. He folded at the middle, sank to his knees, and collapsed onto his face.

Stark felt some of the old sympathetic tension drain out of his shoulders. "Relax," he advised. "It's over; he's not getting up."

For the first time in some minutes he turned his head to look down at the woman seated beside him on the roughhewn bench. She had her dark hair done up in curls beneath a jaunty hat that matched her dark dress. Her well-defined features were lovely even now when they blazed with a righteous anger. Stark found her a lot more appealing than any of the scantier-clad painted women in the crowd. Her determined eyes caught his gaze and held it.

The umpire—they were calling them referees these days—studied his pocket watch as he began to count seconds.

Prudence glanced sharply toward the ring as though to be sure Stark's forecast was correct. Even she must've been able to see that the count was only a formality, but she watched steadily until it came to an end.

"Thirty seconds! The winner, after seventeen rounds!" The referee lifted the victor's hand.

The crowd shifted into motion as the spectators started to leave their seats.

"Come on." Stark rose, offering his arm. "We can find Sload now."

Her hat barely topped his shoulder as he drew her through the ranks of ranchers, businessmen, gamblers, cowboys, and hardcases who rubbed shoulders in the crowd. Some of them had brought their ladies—respectable and otherwise. A scattering of floozies prowled for prey, their made-up faces feral with avaricious hunger.

Stark wondered wryly how he and Prudence fit in with the rest of the crowd. He was dressed fancy in a suit, tooled boots, and a high-dollar Stetson, but he was packing his full regalia of hand weapons just the same. Holstered Colt .45 and sheathed fighting bowie rode his waist like good luck charms, while the little Marlin double-action .38 hideout revolver nestled snugly at the small of his back.

Altogether, he reckoned a top-of-the-line troubleshooter and a feisty lady attorney weren't too out of place in this company, although their business here was of a bit different breed.

Loud opinions were being voiced about the outcome of the fight, while money was starting to change hands as a result of it.

Tony Sload was seated at a rickety table that was

at the center of a bunch of mostly disgruntled spectators. He was handing out some money, but he was
taking in a sight more of it, pausing only to keep
tabs in a tattered little notebook. He must've been
offering the right odds, Stark reflected.

Sload was a toadish man whose soiled, ill-fitting
suit and matching derby might've been taken in part
payment of the debt of some hapless traveling
drummer. He looked more shifty than dangerous,
but he was reputed to tote at least one belly gun on
his slovenly person.

At his back loomed the towering form of an hombre whose face showed he'd spent more than his
fair share of time in the prize ring, and not always
on the giving end of the punches. Stark had seen
him around. He didn't know his name.

"Coming through," Stark advised roughly as they
reached the group clustered about Sload.

Heads turned. Stark saw both surprise and recognition in some of the hard-bitten faces. There was
also ugly appreciation of Prudence's alluring looks,
but the ranks parted before them.

Sload frowned up from his cash box. "Fight's
over, Peacemaker; too late to place a bet."

"I'm not a betting man," Stark said coolly.

"Way I hear it, you're willing enough to bet your
life if somebody pays your price."

"Somebody's paid it." Stark's tone was flat. "You
and I have got business to talk over."

Sload's bulging eyes were wary; Stark's were watchful. He was conscious of Prudence's close presence, of the hostility radiating from some of Sload's customers, and of the brooding gaze of the gambler's pet prizefighter.

"I mean now," he prodded as Sload hesitated. "In private."

Sload leaned back in his flimsy chair and studied Stark gaugingly. Then he reached out and flipped the lid of the cash box shut. "All right, boys," he said bitterly. "Scatter, but don't go far. This better just take a minute," he added to Stark.

"Up to you," Stark told him.

Sload's patrons moved away. Stark didn't cotton to standing with his back to most of the big room. In a crowd this size and of this ilk he was bound to have enemies. He felt a slight touch on his shoulder and knew Prudence had sensed his uneasiness. She'd be watching his back. He'd rather have her doing it than just about anybody else. Still, he shifted a bit to get a wider view of the barn's interior.

Sload's prizefighter hadn't moved.

"Jeb stays," Sload declared.

"Up to you," Stark said again.

"Now, what's your beef?"

"You and me and Miss McKay have a client in common. He came to her for help. She came to me."

"Who are you talking about?"

"Name of Lee Emmers. Drummer from up north. He came to one of your shindigs here and bet on the wrong man. When he came to pay off, you upped the ante on him, nearly doubled it. That's no way to do business, even this sorry kind of business."

"It's the way I have to do it," Sload asserted. "I answer to big people hereabouts, important people. They've got a stake in all my enterprises, a major stake. When they tell me to change the odds then I do it."

Stark shook his head. "Not on a man who's already lost his bet. You don't grandfather him in under your new rules. That's a legal term. The counselor here can explain what it means."

Sload's washed-out face darkened. "I know what it means!"

"You better know what I mean. Emmers paid you off fair and square. You're finished with him. Stick some other loser with your new odds. Cut Emmers free. He does business in these parts; he can't afford to have you or your thugs sniffing down the back of his neck whenever he's hereabouts."

"You heard what I said," Sload protested. "It ain't a good idea to mess with the folks backing me."

"They're not here. I'm messing with you."

"It's not my decision, I'm telling you."

"It is now. Cancel his debt. If he owes any more to your bosses, then take it out of your own percentage or the skimmings you collect off the rest of it."

A hardness had slid in under Sload's puffy features. "Not that easy, Peacemaker."

The words were a signal. Jeb stirred to life and stepped eagerly out from behind the table.

"You're fixing to get yourself hurt," Stark told him coolly. "Sload ain't worth it."

Jeb had three inches on Stark and a good thirty pounds. He stepped closer. "You're the one fixing to take a hurting. I've heard of you. You ain't fought in years."

"Wrong," Stark breathed invitingly. "I just haven't fought where there's rules." He brushed the tail of his coat clear of the butt of his .45.

"I ain't packing iron," Jeb rumbled. "You won't gun down an unarmed man. You'll have to settle this with fists."

Stark sensed Prudence drawing clear. She knew the scent of trouble, as much as she deplored it. With her in the picture, Stark wanted this over with fast.

"With fists?" he murmured. "I reckon not."

Pivoting on his left foot, he stomp-kicked three times with his right—hitting ankle, knee, and thigh, his boot never touching the floor between the kicks. Jeb's leg seemed to buckle in two different directions.

"Well, reckon we'll use fists after all," Stark muttered.

He stepped in and ripped his left hand around once, then twice low into Jeb's meaty side, just under the rib cage. Jeb lurched forward, doubling at the middle. His descending jaw met Stark's uppercutting right two times in quick succession. The force of the second punch carried Stark's elbow all the way past his own ear. It carried Jeb a ways, too. The prizefighter's body seemed to sail backward. He crashed spreadeagled onto the cash table. Both Sload and the piece of furniture were flattened by his limp bulk.

The gambler thrashed beneath the form of his bodyguard. He got one hand free and darted it inside his coat. The metallic click near his ear froze him in mid-grab. He looked up into the barrel of Stark's cocked Colt .45 twelve inches from his face, and steady as a bar in a vise.

"Stick to dealing shaved cards, Sload," Stark advised coldly. "Guns are way out of your territory."

Sload's eyes bulged ever further. He cringed and tried to wriggle backward on the floor, but Jeb's hulk had trapped his legs.

"Here's the way the cards fall," Stark went on. "Any debt Emmers has is canceled. If he runs into more trouble from you or your cronies, I'll see to it that your bosses need a new collection man in Oklahoma Territory. You savvy?"

Excess flesh swelled under Sload's chin as he nodded rapidly. "Sure, Peacemaker. I ain't fixing to deal you crooked on this. You have my word!"

"No," Stark growled. "You have mine."

He let the gambler examine the bore of the .45 for a further span of seconds, then, just for show, which would impress a man of Sload's caliber, he twirled it deftly back into his holster. Straightening, he stepped clear of the tangled pair and offered a crooked elbow to Prudence.

"Miss McKay."

She gave a polite nod and accepted his proffered arm. He felt her fingers dig in tightly, but her face never lost its composure.

The short fracas had attracted some attention, and they had a host of spectators as he escorted her out. But no one tried to block their path, and she handled their exit like an actress leaving the stage.

Outside in the cooler night air she gave a sigh of relief and sagged momentarily against him. He felt the softness of her petite form.

"Thank heaven we're out of that place," she said with feeling.

"Rough crowd," Stark conceded. For a moment in there the deal could've gone against them.

"Next time I'll listen to your advice about attending," she vowed.

She might listen to it, but following it was an altogether different story, Stark reckoned.

He headed the rented buggy back toward the territorial capital of Guthrie, a few miles distant from the makeshift arena. Prudence had seemingly gotten past her moment of weakness. She sat beside him, unspeaking, a shawl across her slender shoulders.

He knew she detested violence even when circumstances made it the only answer. In his profession that was more often than not. He started to break the silence.

Before he could speak up, she anticipated him with that unerring knack she'd acquired of late. "I know it wasn't your fault." Her words and tone were precise.

"Hard to deal with Sload any other way," Stark said. "He'd be a bad apple in any barrel."

"He should be locked up."

"He's slippery as a wet frog; it wouldn't be easy."

"Well, I appreciate you coming out here to help my client."

Stark shrugged. "I likely would've been here anyway," he said without thinking.

Prudence's head swiveled toward him. "Why in the world would you come to a sordid spectacle like that?"

"To see the fight."

"Jim! It's illegal!"

"I don't bet anything. I just watch the action."

"But how can you enjoy such brutality?"

"I cut my teeth on fights of that sort back when

I was in the ring. What you saw tonight was old London-style prizefighting. That was before boxing under the Queensberry rules, with gloves and timed rounds. According to the London rules, a fight went as long as both opponents could continue, and a round ended only when a man was knocked down. Sometimes they'd go sixty, seventy, even over a hundred rounds."

"It's brutal and sadistic to pit men against each other for money or for pleasure." Prudence had gotten her back up.

"It's a sport," Stark stated. "Nothing more. It's athletic competition reduced to its most basic. Men have engaged in it for centuries. The Apostle Paul made reference to it when he spoke of fighting the good fight."

"It's an uncivilized and barbaric practice that's demeaning to everyone, including the spectators!"

"There are rules that raise it above the level of barbarism."

"That's total nonsense. The gladiatorial games in ancient Rome had rules, too!"

"The object there was death. That's not the case in prizefighting."

Prudence shook her head in frustration. "You can rationalize it any way you wish, but it is still illegal, and a God-fearing man shouldn't be patronizing it."

She pretty much had him whipsawed there. "Consider it civil disobedience," he growled. "And just remember, you were quick enough to make use of my experience when it suited your client's needs."

She swung her head toward him, and for an instant the moonlight flashed sparks in her eyes. Then she set her face resolutely to the front, her body as rigid as a fireplace poker.

Stark scowled off across the moonlit prairie. For the first time he noticed the pale silver glow that the shifting face of the half-moon cast across the grassland. The breeze smelled clean and fresh. This was too pretty a night for fussing and squabbling. But once again, like a pair of prizefighters, he and Prudence had managed to find themselves toeing the line for no good reason. Come to think of it, Prudence wouldn't have made a bad prizefighter. Her best combination would've been a one-two to the heart.

He glanced circumspectly at Prudence and fancied that her stiff posture had relaxed a trifle. Had she noticed the beauty of the night as well? He figured he should say something to make amends for his last petty jab at her, but he wasn't in the habit of offering apologies to her, and didn't want to start now. Still, he reckoned he ought to do something.

"Tell your client this one is on the house," he said more gruffly than he'd planned.

She swallowed hard and seemed to have to work to find words. "I'm sure he'll want to compensate you." Her voice had softened.

"Not necessary. An evening with you was payment enough."

She caught her breath, and he saw her trim shoulders relax. "I can think of better ways we could spend the evening," she murmured so softly he barely caught her words.

"Such as?" Stark heard his own hollow tones. Out of the corner of his eye he could see the soft contours of her profile.

"Dinner, the theater, then dancing," she answered softly.

Stark turned to look at her in the same instant as she turned her gaze to him. Her eyes were dark and wide, her face lovely in the moonglow. He knew that like him, she was wondering just where this was headed. Up until now in their tempestuous relationship, they had been careful to ride clear of anything beyond uneasy friendship and business contacts. Were they taking a new trail now?

"You're on," he said.

Chapter One

"Why would Marshal Nix want to see both of us at the same time?" Prudence was puzzled.

"Beats me," Stark drawled. "Could be, he's out to lock us up. What nefarious acts have you been up to lately?"

Prudence looked askance at him, as though suspicious of his rare jocular mood. "Just patronizing prizefights," she said wryly.

"That's it then," Stark declared. "If Evett Nix gets a hold of us, we're headed for the hoosegow. It's my just comeuppance for associating with a law-breaker like you. But I won't go quietly. I'll hit the desperado trail!"

"Don't expect me to ride along," Prudence advised.

14

"Does that include going to the theater this Saturday night?"

"I wasn't aware desperadoes patronized cultural affairs."

"I'll make it my last civilized act before I revert to total barbarism."

Prudence smiled mischievously. "You wouldn't have to revert very far. But I'll risk being around you long enough to hold you to our deal."

A few passersby on the sidewalk were glancing at the picture the two of them made, Stark noticed. And Prudence looked striking even in one of the dark, subdued dresses she favored for her office and the courthouse. Fringes of white lace at the high neck and on the cuffs were the only decorations. Her piquant face was framed by dark curls. Stark had a sudden memory of her with her locks worn loose, tumbling past her shoulders.

He was looking forward to Saturday night when they'd fulfill the pact they'd made after the prizefight. A distant part of his mind knew that it was this anticipation that had briefly overriden his usual sober outlook on the world.

Responding to a missive from U.S Marshal Evett Nix, he had run into Prudence outside the Herriott Building, which held Nix's office. The sidewalks had their usual mix of townsfolk, cowboys, farmers, and Indians. Horsemen, mule-drawn wagons, and horseless carriages vied for space on the cobblestone streets. Guthrie, with its turreted European-style buildings, was a busy cosmopolitan capital, a bit out of place on the untamed plains of Oklahoma Territory.

"You're sure your message said ten o'clock?" Prudence got back to the subject of their unexpected encounter.

"And that he wanted to see me in his office," Stark assured her.

Prudence looked up at a clock mounted in ornate scrollwork. It graced a building across the way housing a surveyor and a bookkeeper in side-by-side offices. "Then we best hurry," she suggested. "It's almost the hour."

"Don't want to keep the law waiting," Stark agreed. He gestured for her to precede him.

As he reached past her to get the door, he caught a quick unreadable glance from her. Then she was past him, the faint flowery scent of her brushing his nostrils.

Evett Nix rose and came from behind his desk as a clerk ushered them into the office. As much businessman as lawman, and more likely to be manning his desk than forking a horse, Nix had been appointed for his administrative skills in organizing the hectic job of law enforcement in Oklahoma Territory.

He had put those skills to good use, and had the common sense to hire experienced lawmen such as

Heck Thomas, Bill Tilghman, and Chris Madsen—
the so-called Three Guardsmen—to advise him on
the peacekeeping function of his job. What had resulted was an efficient and effective organization
that had pitted a small army of U.S. Deputies
against the ranks of outlaws and bandits that
prowled both Oklahoma and the neighboring Indian
lands.

"James, Miss McKay, I'd like you to meet—"
Nix began, but the fourth person in his office was
already rising to stride forward and grip Stark's
hand.

"Stark, it's been a spell."

"For a fact, Bat."

Trim, dapper, handsome despite his years, and
dressed to the nines, he might've been taken by
most folk for a dude from back East—that is, until
hombres who knew had a chance to look in his eyes.
The steel-plated wariness of a mankiller was in
them, a gent who had lived by his wits, by his nerve,
and not least, by his gun.

"I should've known the two of you had crossed
trails at some point," Nix said ruefully.

"Let me introduce Miss Prudence McKay, Attorney and Counselor at Law," Stark took up the formalities. "Prudence, this is William Masterson,
although he favors being called Bat."

"My pleasure, Miss McKay. If the need ever
arises—and unfortunately it might—I'd be honored

to have you represent me in the courtroom." He
bowed gallantly to touch his lips to the back of her
hand.

It was just the right mix of respect and courtli-
ness. Stark could tell that, despite her usual reserve,
Prudence was taken by him.

It came as no great surprise. Gentleman, lawman,
gambler, gunfighter in his younger days, Bat Masterson had walked tall in the booming cowtowns
and cities of the old West. His reputation still cast
a long shadow, and his name carried considerable
weight, although these days he was said to have
hung up his guns.

But he hadn't hung up all of them, Stark saw. He
could tell Bat was toting some kind of shooting iron
in a shoulder rig under his tailored coat.

"Just how did the two of you get to know each
other?" Nix asked.

Stark felt Prudence's questioning eyes on him as
well. He chuckled. "Bat had the dubious honor of
being the referee in the only prizefight I ever had
where I got knocked cold."

Bat's compelling grin flashed. "It never would've
happened, except one of his opponent's cornermen
sandbagged him from outside the ring when he
thought I wasn't looking." Masterson gave a re-
gretful shake of his head. "Of course, then I had to
shoot the sorry scoundrel."

"You killed him?" Prudence gasped in disbelief.

"Nope. I just winged him. Couldn't have those sort of shenanigans going on in a fight when I was the referee. Then I disqualified James's opponent and awarded James the match. When he woke up he wanted to finish the fight."

Prudence gave Stark a look of bemused disapproval before Nix got them all seated in front of his desk. The marshal settled back in his sleek leather swivel chair. As usual his desk was neatly ordered.

"From what I've heard you've ridden quite a few trails since then," Bat addressed Stark. "Pinkerton operative, range detective, lawman, hired gun for worthy causes, and now troubleshooter. 'Peacemaker for Hire.' I like that. It suits you somehow. You always did see yourself as a sort of knight in shining armor."

"Just a sword for hire," Stark said dryly.

Masterson chuckled and withdrew a cigar from within his coat. Then, noting Prudence's wrinkled nose, he returned it to his pocket unlit. Still the gentleman.

"As both of you probably know," Nix broke in, "Bat has become active as a prizefight promoter over the last few years. Technically the sport is illegal in most jurisdictions, but it's still a thriving industry. Even here in the Territory we wink at the so-called exhibitions of self-defense at the sporting clubs." He broke off to acknowledge Prudence's brooding frown of objection. "Exception noted, Prudence. But up until lately I've had bigger fires to put out than a little bit of illicit gambling and fisticuffs."

Prudence had the grace to look slightly chastened; but only slightly. "Apparently something has altered your viewpoint," she observed.

"Yes, it has," Nix admitted. "I know where you stand on the subject in general. I read your recent guest editorial in the newspaper. You state your case well. Would that I had fewer robberies and killings to worry about so that I could devote some of my time to such matters."

It had been their recent visit to the prizefight which had sparked Prudence's fiery editorial debut. Stark had read the piece, and then carefully ridden clear of the topic with Prudence since then.

"I'm also aware of your recent letter to the governor requesting a crackdown on prizefighting," Nix went on. "And I would guess you have petitioned your father to exert some pressure on Washington from his court up in Kansas."

"He happens to be a fan of the so-called self-defense exhibitions," Prudence said tightly. "But you're right; I did try."

"Well, as it happens, your efforts have only added to the concern in Washington. The U.S. Government had been looking into some ugly business that has grown out of the bare-knuckle prizefights."

Stark set his jaw. He had a hunch what was coming. Looked like the dark rumors he'd heard had more than a little basis in truth.

"What kind of business?" Prudence asked.

"They knew I had my hands full as it is." Nix didn't answer her directly. "I asked for some help, and they contacted Mr. Masterson and enlisted him. He's a former law enforcement officer and an expert on prizefighting. He's been appointed a Special U.S. Marshal to ride in tandem with me on this matter."

Masterson was more than suited for the job, Stark reflected. Word was, he had actually turned down an offer to fill the office Nix himself now held.

"I consider myself retired from law enforcement and matters of the gun," Bat took up the reins of the discussion. "I'm content to confine my activities to promoting sports events and doing a little writing for the sports columns in the newspapers."

Stark saw Prudence's lips tighten in obvious irritation at the way Nix and Masterson were dancing around the corral without ever opening the gate. But she refrained from interrupting as Masterson continued.

"There are some activities that are so appalling that I will not countenance them corrupting a sport which I hold near and dear, even beset as it currently is by various legal restrictions and prohibitions."

Stark figured they'd had long enough to show

their hand. "You're talking about the fist-and-boot fights," he said flatly.

"What in the world are those?" Prudence asked sharply.

"No-holds-barred prizefights held in Indian Territory," Stark told her. "They stage them in a big tent that can be moved from site to site. There are no rules; anything goes in the ring. Supposedly a couple of fighters have even been killed in bouts."

"So you're already familiar with it," Nix surmised.

Stark hitched his shoulders. "Just rumors."

"The rumors are true, I'm afraid. Bat has been sent here to put a stop to it."

"Who's responsible for these fights?" Prudence demanded.

"A no-good pair of brothers by the name of Yanger, so we understand," Masterson told her. "Clint and Burt. They were nothing but two-bit gamblers and gunslicks until Clint came up with the notion of holding fights with no referees and no rules, while taking bets on the outcome. He's the brains of the two. Burt, his younger brother, is the enforcer. He's supposed to be the devil on wheels with a pistol. Has six dead men to his credit, all of them in standup gunfights. They've also hired twenty or thirty gun toughs to act as guards and as a work crew to move the tent around."

"They don't sound like the type to be able to run an operation like you've described."

"Clint dreamed up the scheme, but it's gotten larger than just two of them now. They've got backing by a clandestine crime syndicate in the East. There's big money involved. Some of the top dogs in the syndicate are reputed to be more or less respectable businessmen. A lot of the spectators and gamblers are from back East as well. They come out to the Territories just to watch the fights and place their bets. We've heard unconfirmed tales of private trains with Pullman cars loaded down with high rollers from the Eastern cities making the trip out here to bet on the fights."

"This is monstrous!" Prudence exclaimed. The look she gave Stark was almost accusatory. She fixed her attention on the other two men. "You could arrest the Yanger brothers and stop these fights no matter how difficult they are to pin down, and regardless of the fact that they're in Indian Territory. You have jurisdiction there under these circumstances," she charged. "You must want to do more than that. You must want to get the syndicate heads as well."

Masterson looked impressed at her analysis. Nix nodded affirmation.

"That's right," the marshal said, "we do want them. But we've got to get them out here to identify them and prove their complicity in the operation."

"Why rope us in on this?" Stark interjected.

Nix leaned back in his chair, steepled his fingers, and gazed steadily at Prudence. "You've become almost overnight a significant player in the movement to ban prizefighting. You're well known, and respected in the community. Your editorial has become the talk of the town."

"I intend to keep writing on the topic," Prudence asserted. "Especially after what I've learned here today. The editor has invited me to do additional columns."

"We'd appreciate it if you'd see your way clear to refrain from doing that," Nix said very carefully.

Prudence bristled like a cat facing a hound. "I will not be censored by you or—" She broke off abruptly, her usually smooth brow furrowed with thought. "Of course," she said slowly. "You don't want this matter publicized until you've had a chance to lure the backers out here and shut the fights down."

Nix flicked a quick grin at Masterson as though confirming a point. "You're right once more, Prudence," he said aloud. "If there's too much publicity about this, the syndicate bosses will be unwilling to venture out here for any reason."

"I understand. And I'll temper my journalistic efforts for the time being. But don't forget: you are *not* my editor."

"Agreed," Nix said immediately. He appeared relieved.

"That answers the question about my presence here," Prudence pressed on. "But what about Jim? What do you want with him?"

Stark had a moment to experience an unexpected sense of satisfaction at her protective tone. Then Nix gestured at Masterson for a response.

"We need a fighter good enough to force the Yanger brothers to hold a high-stakes bout to lure the syndicate bosses out here," Masterson said. He cocked an inquisitive eyebrow at Stark. "Interested?"

Chapter Two

"Y ou can't ask Jim to do that!" Prudence gasped in outrage. "He'd be risking his life!"

"With all due respect, Miss McKay," Masterson murmured, "that's what he does for a living. We'd compensate him amply for his services."

Prudence started to protest further, then broke off, as if recalling Stark was there and could speak for himself.

There was a time Stark would've resented her butting into his affairs, but he disregarded it now. "That's a mighty tall request," he drawled.

"You were a good fighter back when I first knew you, and since then, I hear, you've become adept at French foot fighting—savate. Wicked stuff."

"Oh, I don't doubt I could do well enough against

most hombres hereabouts," Stark admitted. "But the syndicate boys are bound to have a spoiler tucked away—a professional they'll bring in to lick any fist-and-boot fighter they figure they can't put a harness on. He'd be a former bare-knuckle champ, or a strongarm brawler or jaw buster, but he'd be top notch."

"That's the fight that would bring the bosses out here in person," Masterson agreed. "You'd have to be set to go against their spoiler, but hopefully we'd move in and shut down the operation before it became necessary to actually fight him."

"Hopefully," Stark echoed, but he wasn't sure he actually meant it. There was no experience—none—like facing off against another man in the ring. How good was he these days? he asked himself. Had he lost the old skills that had been his meal ticket in his younger years? Since then his experience and his ability with a gun had earned him a rep that commanded top dollar. Had he come to rely too much on the guns and other weapons he wielded in his profession?

"You're well known enough to attract a lot of interest once word gets out that you'll be in the ring," Nix said. "Folks would pay to see you, and they'd sure enough be willing to place bets on you, win, lose, or draw."

Prudence was glaring at Stark as if she could sense which trail he was fixing to ride.

"You'd be reporting to me, but our contacts would have to be circumspect," Masterson explained. "You'll be on your own much of the time."

That was hardly new, Stark reflected. He couldn't quite figure Prudence's displeasure. Heaven knew, she'd enlisted him in more than one cause where he'd ended up risking his life. And, like Masterson had reminded her, that was part and parcel of the trouble trade.

But something besides the unholy urge to pit himself against another man was spurring him as well. "I don't cotton to this type of business going on in prizefighting," he said aloud. "One day it'll become respectable. The fist-and-boot matches are degrading to the sport and to the fighters themselves." He glanced pointedly at Prudence. "There's your true barbarism, your true throwback to the Roman gladiators." He switched his gaze to the two men. "If I can lend a hand in stopping it, I'm more than willing."

"Excellent!" Nix exclaimed. Masterson grinned a tight gambler's grin. Stark avoided looking at Prudence.

"Now that we have that settled, there is one more issue." Nix shifted uneasily.

Prudence left off her baleful regard of Stark to eye the lawman. "Go on."

"As I mentioned, Prudence has become well known to the public as an advocate for the prohibition of prizefighting, or, rather, the more active enforcement of the existing laws." Nix was choosing his words like a man would pick his steps in a bed of rattlers, Stark thought.

"Also," Nix went on, "the two of you are fairly well known to be—" He broke off as two pairs of wary eyes nailed him suspiciously. "—acquaintances," he finished carefully.

Stark and Prudence relaxed only a trifle. Nix cleared his throat and plowed manfully on. "In order for Stark's decision to take up illegal prizefighting to be believable, there will need to be some sort of fairly public break between the two of you. Then your contact with one another should be strictly curtailed until this job is over." He stopped and awaited reactions.

For a moment he got none. Then Stark opened his mouth to object, but Prudence beat him to the punch.

"That shouldn't be difficult to arrange," she said coolly. "We'll have a fine stage for it Saturday night. We have a dinner engagement."

Stark looked at her in surprise. For an instant he fancied he detected a spark of regret, quickly squelched, far back in her dark eyes. Then they turned as cool as her voice.

After that, Stark avoided her gaze.

But there was no avoiding the matter once they'd left the marshal's office. "I don't want you to do this, Jim!" she exclaimed, unleashing her pique with him.

Stark stopped. He towered over her. For the moment they had the hallway to themselves. "Figured you'd be in favor of anything to shut down prizefighting," he said shortly.

"I'm opposed to prizefighting, but I'm also opposed to you getting hurt or killed!"

"Can't say I'm in favor of it," he drawled. "But the risk goes with the territory."

Her full lips thinned. "It doesn't have to, not this time."

Stark shrugged. "It ain't your decision."

He made to turn away, but her hand caught his arm with a compelling grip. "Are you doing this just because I object to it?" she demanded.

Stark snorted. "Don't give yourself that much credit. I meant what I said in there. Those bouts are an ugly business. They need to be stopped."

"Is that the only reason?" she persisted. "What are you trying to prove?"

Stark was beginning to wish he was in the ring with some bare knuckle opponent rather than squaring off with her. "Anything I ever had to prove to anybody, I've proved a long time ago," he said roughly.

"So you just keep on trying to prove it to yourself!" she accused.

Stark gave a single exasperated shake of his head.

"What put this burr under your saddle?" he demanded rather than face her question. "Looks to me like we're on the same side of this. The danger's never bothered you too much before when you recruited me to be in some cause or another."

Her eyes grew suddenly bright with moisture. "It's always bothered me a great deal!" she asserted with soft intensity. "But all the other times there's only been the possibility of danger. This time it's much more than that. This time there's the certainty that you'll have to fight for your life in the ring against someone who may be younger than you, or a better fighter, or in better shape, or all of those things!"

"I reckon I know where your money will be riding," Stark growled. "Don't count me out before the bell's even been rung."

"I'm just afraid of what will happen after it does ring!"

Another draw, Stark mused bleakly. At least in the ring there was usually a winner.

He escorted her back to her office in a strained silence.

"I'll pick you up at six on Saturday night," he advised stiffly at her office door.

She looked back up at him over her shoulder and gave a rueful smile. "I'll be ready."

She was gone before he could answer.

Stark shook his head again. Try as he would, he

didn't figure he'd ever make heads or tails out of her.

Moodily he left the building and strode over to his office. At the door he heard a scurrying of footsteps behind him and came swiftly about.

"Whoa up, Peacemaker! I need to see you!"

Stark relaxed slightly. He cocked his head skeptically. "Sload, what in blazes are you doing on the law-abiding side of town?"

The squat gambler looked even more disheveled than he had the night of the fight. His jowled features were half angry and half worried. Stark could smell stale alcohol and fresh sweat.

"I need to talk to you, Stark. It's important. You owe me!"

Stark was leery. He recollected Sload's hideout gun and hired strongarm man. But the gambler looked to be alone. "What's got you snorting?" Stark prodded.

"Let's go in your office. You think I want to be seen palavering with you?"

Keeping him in the edge of his vision, Stark unlocked the door. It didn't seem to have been tampered with, and Sload pushed eagerly through the portal once it was open, showing no concern over what might lie within.

Stark followed him and heeled the door shut.

Sload didn't waste time. "You butting in with me

over that sorry mark the other night could've brought me a heap of trouble!" he declared.

"How's that? Your bosses upset that your take is down?" Stark guessed aloud.

"Yeah, they're upset, and it don't look to get any better. The way you crippled up Jeb left me without protection. Half of the betters who owed me money just walked out. And the word's got around that I'm some kind of jinx or something. Nobody's placing bets with me. They figure that since I got crossways of you, my time's limited anyway. Hang you for a meddler, Stark!"

"You're wasting my time," Stark said. "Don't expect me to cover your crooked bets or go around trying to collect them." He resisted the impulse to boot the gambler back out the door. Now that he thought about it, maybe there was a way he could use Sload.

"I figure you owe me for what you done to my operation," Sload blustered.

Stark hitched a hip onto one corner of his desk. "Just what are you getting at?"

Sload drew a deep breath. He seemed a little shaken that Stark was willing to lend him an ear. "If things get much worse, there'll be folks who want answers, and they'll send men looking for me, men who know how to get those answers. That'll be when I need you."

"To protect your sorry tail?" Stark inquired dryly.

"If it comes to that, yeah!"

Stark bit back the sneering response that rose automatically to his lips. He sat there for a moment chewing things over. Here was a door opening to him; no reason not to go through it.

"Maybe we can do business," he said casually.

Sload gulped like a toad that had just swallowed a June bug. "You mean you'd back me if trouble comes my way?" Pretty clearly he hadn't been expecting much from Stark, which meant he must figure himself to be in a pretty tight spot, to come here looking for help.

So much the better.

"Let's just say you may need my help, and I may need a little something in return."

"I can't pay your high-dollar wages!" Sload groused. "I done told you already—you put the ax to anybody placing bets through me."

"I need information," Stark told him.

Sload eyed him with the instinctive suspicion of a chiseler figuring he might be the one about to be chiseled. "What kind of information?"

"Suppose a fellow wanted to make a little money in the fight business?"

"Shoot, Peacemaker, I can take your bets."

"I wasn't talking about putting money on somebody else's man," Stark said deliberately.

Sload's eyes widened. "You mean you got a fighter of your own?"

"Like Jeb?" Stark jeered. "I'm no manager or promoter, leastways not unless I'm promoting myself."

Now Sload's eyes bulged. "Are you talking about yourself? You want to get back in the prize ring?"

"I'm just like a cat with a mouse," Stark advised. "I'm playing with the notion."

Sload's fleshy throat heaved as he swallowed. "You give me the word and I can set you up real nice," he vowed. "Folks would sure be willing to put down money to see the Peacemaker fight!" He blanched and broke off. "Mind you," he cautioned uneasily. "We got rules, old English-style rules: fists and wrassling throws are permitted, but none of that fancy kick fighting you used on Jeb."

"I don't need kick fighting to put a man down for the count."

Sload nodded nervously, then scowled as another thought came to him. "But ain't you keeping time with that lady who has everybody so fired up over banning prizefighting?"

"She don't hold my reins," Stark gritted ominously.

Oily sweat popped out of the pores on Sload's face. "Sure, sure, Peacemaker," he stammered. "Ain't nobody saying otherwise!"

Stark nailed him in place with a glare for a pair of seconds, then straightened off the corner of the desk. "Scat!" He jerked his head toward the door.

"But what about—?"

"You get word to me if trouble comes down the pike. We'll talk about the other when I figure the time's right."

Stark wrinkled his nose once the gambler had scrambled clumsily from his office. The odor of decay still seemed to hang in the air.

He'd offered the bait and Sload had taken it. Now wasn't the time to land him. There was still some groundwork to be laid, not the least of which was to take place Saturday night. After that, for all the public knew, he and Prudence McKay would no longer be—what had Nix called it? Yeah, *associates*.

Chapter Three

She was as gentle as an Oklahoma breeze in his arms as he swept her around the dance floor. He marveled at the lightness of her step and the softness of her petite form. He himself moved his feet with gliding smoothness he would use in the prize fight ring, or in performing a savate sequence, but her gracefulness made him feel as awkward and clumsy as a trained bear. Still, he knew they moved well together, flowing with the lift and turn of the music. He knew too that she made a breathtaking image in an ivory gown with a beribboned neckline that scooped a bit lower than was her wont.

At some point she had nestled her brunette curls against his vest, and it was a pressure that was at once enticing and unnerving. He couldn't resist tilting his head to gaze down at her. Sensing his movement perhaps, she lifted a flushed face to him and he let himself delve the hazel depths of her eyes.

Dimly, with disappointment, he heard the music end. He swirled her to a halt, reluctant to release her from the circle of his arms.

There was a smattering of applause. Stark glanced about and realized with a sense of shock that most of the other folk on the dance floor had drawn back, forming a ring of spectators inside which he and Prudence had been performing.

"Oh mercy," Prudence gasped as she took in the situation. Then she looked up at Stark with a gamine twinkle in her eyes.

Somehow Stark grasped her intent instantly. As she turned to perform a flawless curtsy to the makeshift audience, he joined her with a deep bow. They were both laughing with the sheer pleasure of it as they returned to their table.

They'd dined at the Vienna Restaurant, lingering over rich desserts from the bakery and confectionery. The Brooks Theatre presented a melodramatic tale of young lovers separated by events, only to be ultimately reunited after many trials and tribulations. Seated close beside Stark, Prudence had seemed enthralled. He'd had trouble keeping his mind off her and on the performance.

The ballroom offered ginger ale among its beverages, and they sipped the bubbly liquid from their glasses as the band rested between numbers. He'd never tasted anything so sweet, Stark thought.

Setting his glass down he leaned back and grinned fondly across the table. "Who would've believed it?" he wondered. "All evening and nary a cross word between us."

"That's surely some sort of a milestone," Prudence agreed with a pleased smile of her own. Then a shadow seemed to cross over her face. "It's a shame"—she sighed wistfully—"that our wonderful evening together has to end the way it will."

Stark glanced about the crowded ballroom. "At least they'll remember us," he predicted dryly.

Like her he was feeling a deep regret that the evening was destined to finish with a staged argument between them. But even deeper ran a perverse sense of relief. They had spent the entire evening without any of their usual squabbles or spats. He wasn't sure he wanted to know where this trail they rode might have taken them. Would it have ended in commitments neither of them were really ready or willing to make?

Or were they ready after all and just unwilling to admit it?

"Well," Prudence said with determination. "Here it goes." She pressed her fingertips against the linen tablecloth as if to rise.

"Whoa." Stark forestalled her with an open palm. "I'll play the villain."

"Such a gentleman," she said wryly, but made no objection.

"You shouldn't have a problem hiring a hansom to take you home," Stark went on in a low voice. "And I arranged with Nix to have a man standing by outside to be sure you don't run into trouble."

"My, how did I ever get along without you?" she asked archly. "But I am flattered. I doubt any girl has ever had a man take such elaborate precautions to see to her safety before he walks out on her."

"I'd wager no hombre's ever been fool enough to walk out on you before now."

She blushed as pink as a rose, but gave her head a sportish toss. "I just hope my reputation can handle it. Of course any lady who has her escort desert her can hardly be faulted with finding someone to replace the boor." She let her gaze rove speculatively over the other males in the room. More than one of them had fruitlessly sought a turn on the dance floor with her.

"I'd break his arms," Stark warned. "Then I'd pull out his teeth and stuff them up his nose."

"Jim!" Prudence gasped in a mixture of horror and barely suppressed mirth. "That's awful!"

"That's nothing. You ought to see me when I'm in the ring."

"That I don't plan to do," Prudence said soberly.

"Reckon it's time we started this rodeo." Stark pushed his chair back and rose. As he did he swung his arm in a backhanded sweep that carried both their glasses from the table to shatter on the hardwood floor.

"I'll do what I blasted please, woman!" he snarled with enough volume and savagery to make Prudence blink in spite of herself. "You don't pull my reins! Understand?"

Prudence shot to her feet. Her tone matched Stark's in fervor. Plainly she had quickly gotten into the spirit of things. "How dare you talk to me that way!"

"I'll talk to you any blamed way I please! And I'll do anything I blamed well like, including stepping into the prize ring!"

"Well, go right ahead! And I hope you get your silly head knocked off! It would serve you right!"

Stark knew they were more the center of attention now than they'd ever been when dancing. He hoped all the onlookers were getting an earful. And Prudence was doing a fine enough job of acting to make him wonder if there weren't some genuine feelings behind her words.

"There's nobody in these parts can whip me—in the ring or out!" he raged. "And I don't need you trying to run my life!"

"Believe me, I don't want any part of the life of a—a prizefighter!"

"Suits me just fine!"

Stark figured they'd gotten the point across. It

wasn't much fun brawling with Prudence, even
when neither of them meant what they said. Or did
they? At some point he'd stopped being quite sure.

Disquieted, he stalked from the ballroom. The
scowl on his face was only partly for show. He
could feel the disapproving eyes of just about everybody in the place, but his glare warned off any in-
terference.

Outside, the night air felt cool on his face. The
hour was late, but he was in no mood for calling it
a day. Now was as good a time as any to push
things along.

Gas street lamps cast pools of light along the
sidewalks. Only a few horsemen clattered past on
the cobblestones of the street.

By habit Stark stayed to the shadows as he
headed toward the railroad tracks. Before he reached
the west edge of the downtown district he could see
the lights and hear the sounds of the Reaves Brothers Casino.

On the other side of the street the notorious Blue
Belle Saloon was also still in full swing. Stark
guessed the bar was being put to regular use tonight.

The Reaves Brothers Casino was a fancy three-
story structure that served as a watering hole for
professional sporting men and any other folks interested in trying their hands at games of chance.
Since there were no prizefights outside of town tonight, Stark figured it was a pretty good bet he'd

find his quarry there along with the rest of the gaming crowd.

A handful of rowdies drew back as he neared the door. Business was brisk inside. Sharp-eyed gunslicks, hardscrabble farmers, suited drummers, and politicians along with dusty cowpokes vied with the house on games of chance ranging from hazard to craps to assorted card games. Pool balls clicked together, roulette wheels turned, and Liberty Bell slot machines whirred. A piano played in the background. Painted women circulated in the crowd, available on demand.

Stark threaded his way through the ranks, eyes narrowed against the stinging haze of tobacco smoke and whiskey fumes. The garish music was jarring after the smooth strains of the band in the ballroom.

Tony Sload was just fixing to toss a small disk at the gaping mouth of a metal toad in a round of *el sapo* when Stark stepped deliberately into his line of vision. Sload glimpsed him as he made his toss. Stark's hand flicked out and closed on the disk in midair. He dropped it to disappear beneath the feet of the other players. There was some uncharitable laughter.

At least there were plenty of witnesses around to spread word of his meeting with Sload, Stark mused wryly.

Sload cursed. "Hang you, Stark! What the deuce are you doing butting in here?"

"Thought I might bring you some luck."

"Shoot! Thanks to you I just lost my shirt on that throw. Some luck!"

"I wasn't talking about a game," Stark said deliberately.

Sload's bulging eyes narrowed hungrily. He elbowed his way clear of the other players. "Come on, let's talk." He reached for Stark's elbow.

Wordlessly Stark shifted his arm clear.

"Sorry," Sload said hastily. "Over here. We can have some privacy."

Sload led him to a small room with a table and chairs intended for private games. That fitted the use they were putting it to, Stark decided.

Sload found glasses and a bottle in a cupboard. He poured for himself, then frowned as Stark waved off his offer. "In training, huh?" he surmised.

Stark didn't waste time. "I'm ready to fight." He jabbed a finger across the table at Sload. "I hear you can set things up."

"Sure, I already told you that." Sload was so eager he put his whiskey aside untasted. "You saw our little shindig the other night. We set those up every couple of weeks."

Stark shook his head. "I ain't interested in some bare-knuckle square dance."

"But you said you was interested in fighting!"

"That isn't fighting, not real fighting." Stark stared hard at him.

Sload licked his lips. Now he did belt down his drink. "What are you talking about?"

Stark jerked his head impatiently. "Don't waste my time! If I'm climbing back into the ring, I want it to be worth my while. There's a lot more dinero to be had fighting than what I'd get out the kind of match you're talking about."

Sload's thick mouth twisted cynically. "You're known for running with the law dogs. I ain't sure I can trust you."

Stark laughed harshly. "I'm known even more for fighting for money. You think I'm interested in bringing the law down on you? Where's my gain in that? You see me regular at the bare-knuckle fights. I'm a longtime patron, you know that. I've got no reason to work with law on this. Shoot, most lawmen just wink at prizefighting anyway."

"These ain't no ordinary prizefights we're talking about now." Sload poured and drank again, spilling some in the process. "I'll have to see what I can do."

"Just put in a word for me with your bosses, the Yanger boys. Don't worry, I'll make it worth your while."

"When you fight fist and boot it can be for keeps."

There—it was out in the open at last. Stark

laughed again. "I've killed more than one man in bare-handed fights that weren't in a ring. It doesn't get any rougher than that." The boast left a bitter taste in Stark's mouth for all that it was true.

But Sload finally seemed convinced. His jowls bulged as he nodded. "I'll set up a meet." Emboldened, he added, "Now you and I got to talk terms."

"I'm my own manager and promoter," Stark said. "I'll cut you in for ten percent as my agent."

Sload's jowls puffed up. "That ain't much."

Stark shrugged. "Take it or hit the trail. I'll track down the Yanger boys on my own eventually. And when I do, I'll tell them you tried to keep me from having a palaver with them. You'll be in even bigger trouble than you are now."

Much of Sload's boldness drained away. "Sure, all right. I'll get word to you on a meet with them."

"Don't keep me waiting or I'll get impatient." Stark kicked his chair back as he rose. Glancing coldly over his shoulder, he left the room.

The gaming tables held no appeal for him. Back out in the cleansing night air he headed for the Royal Hotel where he leased his suite. No one followed him from the casino.

He'd taken the first step down a dangerous trail, he reflected, and he didn't trust his guide any more than a cardsharp's promise. But he'd see where the trail led just the same.

In his rooms he'd barely shucked his coat, string

tie, and hideout .38 when a quick tapping sounded on the door. He fisted his Colt and stepped to the panel, careful to stay clear of it. "Sing out," he growled.

"Open up," came a familiar voice, followed by another peremptory tap.

Stark opened the door just as Bat Masterson lowered the gold-headed walking stick he'd used to knock.

Chapter Four

"Saw you come in," the dapper gambler said as he slipped past Stark into the suite. "I waited a few minutes to be sure no one saw me follow you. It's not a good idea for us to be seen together."

Stark holstered his Colt. He felt a moment's chagrin that he'd missed Masterson's presence outside. But at least he'd been taken by an old pro at the game.

Masterson flicked his derby onto the hat tree and strolled into the living room, glancing about with apparent approval. He twirled his cane with an unconscious ease. Stark had heard that he'd taken up using a cane when recovering from wounds in a gunfight early in his career. His opponent had never had a chance to recover.

As a lawman Bat had become handy at using his walking stick to buffalo troublemakers before even the fastest of them could get a gun unlimbered. His knack for laying hombres out in such fashion had earned him the sobriquet which he'd carried ever since. The gold-headed cane he sported now had been awarded to him by the grateful citizens of old Dodge City. He looked as if he hadn't yet lost skill at handling the unorthodox weapon.

Masterson stopped by the window, but not in front of it. He peered out at the city lights and shook his head in wonder. "Guthrie's sure not the same town it was last time I was here," he commented.

"You mean when you were a streetcleaner?" Stark said wryly.

Bat chuckled and turned away from the window. "Reckon you might call it that." He nodded in remembrance. "Some folks have gotten my brother mixed up with me as having been here. It wasn't long after the Land Run. There was nothing but an ocean of tents in mud ankle deep. Nobody was willing to give up the place they'd staked a claim, and every man jack of them was armed to the teeth and ready to fight anybody who challenged their right to be there. A wilder sea of iniquity I've never laid eyes on: saloons, bawdy houses, gambling halls all operating in tents."

Stark listened silently, recalling those wild days himself.

"A city government of sorts was set up, and streets were laid out on paper. Then Bill Tilghman and me, as peace officers, were given orders to see that those streets got laid out for real. Right at first he couldn't figure just how we were supposed to do that. Then we put our heads together and came up with a notion.

"We brought in two big logs, wide enough laid end to end, for a decent-sized avenue. We chained them together, hitched a foursome of mules at either end, then gave fair warning we were coming through. Each of us rode in front of one of the mule teams. We were decked out each with a pair of sixes and a saddle gun in plain sight, and we were plumb ready to use them.

"At the designated hour we started those mules moving. Anything in the path of those logs got flattened into the mud. There were folks running for cover, or pulling up pegs and trying to haul their tents clear. Some made it; some didn't, but we darn sure had city streets laid out before we were finished." He grinned. "Reckon they had the numbers and firepower to stop us if they were of a mind to, but none of them wanted to be the first martyr to the cause."

His reminiscing finished, Masterson abandoned the window, settled into one of the easy chairs and regarded Stark pensively. Some age was showing in his face and hair, but his chin still carried its aggressive thrust, and his pale gray eyes beneath the dark brooding brows still carried the same impact as when he and Tilghman had backed down an entire city of hardcases.

Age or not, Stark wouldn't have cared to tangle with him.

"I thought I'd drop by and see how the performance went," Masterson explained.

Stark winced, remembering Prudence's tone and words. They had stung even though their squabble had been staged. "It was a rousing success from where I stood."

Masterson listened as he recounted the evening's events, finishing with his visit to the casino and his meeting with Sload.

"You work fast," Masterson remarked. "Do you believe this Sload character is tied to the Yanger brothers?"

"I've heard they use him and the bareknuckle bouts to recruit fighters for the Fist and Boot matches. I think I can use him to get my foot in the door."

"This is an ugly affair," Masterson declared bleakly. "I've served as umpire—excuse me, they're calling it referee nowadays—in a good number of fights, and I've promoted a good number more. I hate to see even the bareknuckle bouts still going on. It sets the fight industry back at a time when it's gaining increasing acceptance among the public. There's promoters like Matt Stuart, who's haring around trying to get a fight between Fitzimmons and Maher recorded for moving pictures. That's sure to attract more fans. And now with the Queensberry rules and the wearing of gloves pretty well accepted, as well as a civilized scientific fighter like Jim Corbett as heavyweight champion, you'll see the injuries go down. That will ultimately lead to legislation to legalize and regulate the fight game." He broke off and shook his head. "What's your next move?"

"Prod Sload until I get an invite to meet with the Yanger boys, then push them to let me fight."

"Evett and I will be standing by. The big problem is still how you plan to get word to us before you're in the ring with some bruiser looking to stomp you to death. This whole deal could go lickety-bang and blow up in our faces if we're not careful."

"I take a lot of stomping," Stark said, but he'd been mulling the same problem. Sload couldn't be trusted as even an unwilling ally if he ever learned Stark's true purpose in getting in the ring again. "I'll just have to play each hand as it's dealt," he said aloud.

"If you do flush the ringleaders from back East, don't underestimate them," Bat advised. "They'll have top-notch protection. Gunfighting and fast draws aren't confined strictly to the West. I've seen a few Eastern guns I'd lay even money on against just about any hombre. Of course you know this from your days as a Pinkerton, but most of them favor a shoulder rig." He flipped the lapel of his coat back to reveal a brief glimpse of leather and nickel-plated steel beneath his arm.

"Colt Peacemaker with a short barrel," Stark said laconically.

"You have a sharp eye." Deliberately Masterson dipped his hand inside his coat and drew the pistol. "I ordered it special from Colt," he advised. "You aren't the only one who favors the Peacemaker, although I had this one made with a short barrel to accommodate a shoulder rig."

Stark accepted the gun, careful not to let it point toward its owner. He examined the weapon. The barrel was the same length as the ejector rod, which would cut down on its accuracy at any distance, but would make it both quicker to bring into play and more deadly at close quarters. The pearl handle meant less traction for the hand in pulling it, but it suited Bat's fancy style of dress.

Gently he earred the hammer back. The mechanism worked smoothly. He guessed the bents on the hammer as well as the mainspring had been altered to make cocking and firing easier. Thumb on the hammer, he pulled the trigger and eased it back down.

"Nice for speed at close range," he commented.

Bat grinned. "I haven't had much need for a long

gun since I hunted buffalo and fought the Indians at Adobe Wall. Let's see that blunderbuss you carry."

Respectfully Stark returned the pistol and proffered the long-barreled Peacemaker which had earned him his own sobriquet.

Masterson looked it over thoughtfully, equally careful not to cover its owner. "Not much customizing," he remarked.

"Never went in much for that sort of thing."

"I hear you. Customizing is fine, but all the modifications in the world won't help unless the man using the gun has courage, nerve, and skill with the weapon." He broke off and grinned. "And of course it always helps to shoot first and never miss."

He passed the Colt back to Stark and rose to his feet. "I'll be moseying along. Do your best to keep us informed. We'll do everything we can, without exposing you, to keep tabs on your coming and going."

"Don't cover me too close. They'll be suspicious enough as it is."

"Keno." Masterson set his derby on his head, tilting it at a rakish angle. "We'll be the soul of discretion." He reached for the doorknob.

"One other thing," Stark said almost grudgingly.

Bat paused. "What's that?"

"I'd count it a favor if you'd keep an eye on Prudence—Miss McKay. She's headstrong as a mustang, and I don't like her being mixed up in this business."

Masterson studied him, a twinkle in his eye. "Something going on here?"

"I just don't want to see anything happen to her," Stark answered tersely.

Masterson sobered. "The lady impresses me as being able to take care of herself. But I'll lend my talents to doing the same."

"Obliged."

Masterson touched the gold head of his cane to the brim of his derby and slipped from the suite. The door closed softly behind him.

Gun dangling from his fist, Stark stared moodily after him. Masterson had managed to stop riding the trouble trail for the most part, he mused. So had Bat's onetime fellow lawman, Wyatt Earp. Neither of them made a living with the gun these days. Could be that was why both of them were still alive while Hickock, Ringo, Thompson, and others from the old days had gone down under the gun.

Not many men grew old in this trade, Stark knew. Would he himself have the sense to hang up his guns when time slackened his skills? Did he even want to?

Masterson's eyes had lit up when he spoke of the wild days when Guthrie was young. Did he ever miss the taste of danger? Stark suspected that he did.

He dropped the Colt back in its holster. Gratefully he shed his vest then shrugged out of his shirt.

A tentative knock came from the door.

Headed for the bedroom, Stark drew up. He tossed the shirt aside and once more fisted the Colt. Tonight must be his night for folks to come calling. But who in blazes could this be? He snapped open the door, Colt leveled.

Prudence McKay shrank back with a gasp. Stark hastily holstered the Colt, fumbling for words.

She beat him to the punch. "I wanted—I had to come see you," she managed breathlessly. "I had Evett's man escort me over. He's waiting." She lowered her eyes then, finding them resting on Stark's bare chest, lifted them quickly to his face.

She had changed out of her ballroom gown to a more modest dress, and pinned her curls up. Her left hand kept a nervous grip at the shawl draped over her slender shoulders. A flush touched her becoming features in the light of the hallway's oil lamps.

Still bemused, Stark made an awkward gesture to invite her in.

"No!" she said in a rush. "I must go. But I didn't want to part the way we did, even if it was all an act."

"I didn't like it either." Stark's voice was hoarse.

Her eyes shone. "Take care of yourself. Please." She lifted her hand to his chest in that familiar intimate gesture that was part caress and part restraint. This time her fingers brushed his flesh.

He caught his breath at her touch. She too seemed to flinch at the contact. Turning, she fled down the hall.

After a moment Stark shut the door. Sweating, he crossed to open the window.

Chapter Five

Sweat coursed down Stark's bare shoulders and the sculpted contours of his torso. The big canvas bag of sawdust jerked and swung on its chain beneath the sledging impacts of his fists. Soaking in brine over the last several days had toughened the already thick hide of his hands to a leathery texture. Even the repeated blows on the bag's rough fabric didn't skin his knuckles.

He wasn't alone in the old gymnasium. Other fighters pounded bags, sparred, or loafed indifferently. They were a rough crew. Stark's role as a prizefighter had brought him here to this old converted barn on the edge of the prairie just outside of Guthrie. It smelled of dirt, sweat, and liniment.

The shades of beaten fighters long forgotten seemed to hover in the dusty haze.

"I got us a fight!" Sload's voice butted in on Stark's single-minded battering of the bag.

He brought his right around in one last hooking punch that sank his fist wrist-deep. The bag buckled and seemed to gasp beneath the force of the blow.

With it still dancing crazily on its chain, Stark turned away. "I reckon what you mean is that you got *me* a fight," he drawled.

"Same thing," Sload said with an oily grin. "We're partners."

Stark would sooner have been partners with a rattler, but he didn't voice the thought. "So when do I get to meet the Yanger boys?"

Sload licked his lips. "There's a catch."

At his sides Stark's big hands clenched once more into fists. "Spit it out."

"Like a gesture of good faith, since you've never fought for them before," Sload explained hurriedly. "They want you to have one bare-knuckle bout before you toe the mark to fight fist and boot."

"That wasn't the deal," Stark said flatly.

"You've got to do it this way if you want a shot at the high-dollar payoff. One fight, and if you win it, then we talk to them. They're interested, mighty interested. But they want to see you in action first, and make sure you're willing to ride the whole distance."

Stark didn't figure he had much choice, and in fact he wasn't too displeased with this bit of progress. "When?" he demanded in surly tones.

"Saturday night."

"Set it up." Stark glanced about the room. There were plenty of ears that might overhear what was being said. "We'll talk over the details later."

Sload grinned his greasy grin. "Sure thing," he promised, then turned and gestured another man forward. "This here's Thomas Sampson. He'll be your corner man. He'll give you the lowdown on your opponent."

Thomas was the dusky, curly-haired boxer Stark had watched lay out his taller foe with body blows on the night he and Prudence had attended the fights.

The stocky prizefighter ambled forward, eyeing Stark with amiable curiosity. He gave a nod of greeting. Stark stuck out his hand and found it caught in a grip he had to strain to match.

After a span of heartbeats Thomas let up on the pressure, although Stark knew he hadn't bested the other man in the test of strength.

"Obliged to meet you, Mr. Stark." Thomas beamed.

"Make it Jim." Stark worked his hand. "And from

now on let's just nod when we meet," he added dryly.

Thomas chuckled and flexed his own fingers. "Might not be a bad idea," he allowed.

"Take good care of him, Thomas," Sload ordered.

"Yes sir, Mr. Sload."

The gambler waddled off toward a lean youngster attacking a small bag with more determination than skill. Stark hoped that the youth had another career as a backup.

"Saw you fight the other evening," Stark said then to Thomas. "Nice job."

"Thanks. That was the win I needed to get a shot at fighting fist and boot. It's what I been working toward for a spell now."

"Not many rules from what I hear."

"Main rule is winning."

"Fighting a man that way in front of folks bother you?"

Thomas frowned. "Been fighting all my life, one way or another, most times without rules. May as well be doing it for a big payoff, is the way I look at it."

Stark could see the scars of some of those battles etched in Thomas's dark face. He had taken a rare immediate liking to the other man, and the notion of him being a player in this ugly game didn't set well. Thomas seemed like a decent sort of hombre.

But he'd done enough prying. "Who am I fighting Saturday night?" he asked.

"Yahoo by the name of Hammer Jones. He's fought fist and boot himself a couple of times, so they say. Let's go next door, get us something to drink, and I'll tell what I know about him."

Next door was a rundown cross between eatery and saloon, catering to the riffraff that populated this side of the tracks. In the late morning it was deserted except for a drunk and a table of shabby poker players. The game looked to have been going on all night. All the players looked to be losers.

Stark sipped coffee while Thomas smacked his lips over a beer. "I've heard tell you did some fighting in the old days," Thomas remarked once he'd set his mug down.

"A little."

"So this ain't exactly new to you."

"Nope. We'll be fighting London rules, right?"

"Yep." Thomas nodded. "No gloves, knockdowns and wrestling throws allowed, but no kicking, gouging, biting, choking, head butts, or low blows. A round ends when a man goes down. He has thirty seconds to toe the mark."

"Tell me about Hammer Jones."

"Big ornery cuss. Got his nickname from pounding on folks this way." Thomas banged the edge of his clenched fist down on the table. "Seen him durn near drive a man through the floor of the ring that way. He's as much of a wrestler as a boxer howsomever, and he likes to butt when he can get away with it."

So the test wasn't going to be a cakewalk, Stark reflected. If Jones had already graduated from the bare knuckle bouts to fighting fist and boot, then he wasn't any greenhorn in the ring. The Yanger boys wanted to see what their new man was made of. A rep from the old days wasn't enough.

Thomas had leaned back in his rickety chair and was regarding Stark curiously. "Answer me this, will you?"

"Shoot."

"What's a top-dollar gun hawk like yourself doing getting mixed up in this kind of mess?"

"*You're* in it," Stark countered.

"Difference is I ain't no gunfighter. I fight with these." He displayed his big scarred fists. "I'm not saying I necessarily favor staging fights like this, but I figure I might make enough to get my own place and settle down. Nothing much—just a little house and a few acres. Maybe I'll send for a gal down south who's been waiting for me."

"I make my living fighting," Stark took his turn. "Guns or fists or knives, makes no difference. Just so happens I can make more money fighting with my fists than I can with my guns right now, if what I hear is right."

"Yeah, and you might get your head knocked off in the bargain."

"Or blown off if I'm using my guns." Stark shrugged. "Goes with the territory."

"You sound like a mighty hard man," Thomas said almost sadly. "Ain't there nothing you've got to look forward to except fighting and killing?"

Stark recollected the glow in Masterson's eyes when he recalled his old days of glory. Then the memory was dispelled by an image of hazel eyes in a piquant face framed by dark curls.

He gave his head an irritated shake to clear it. Thomas was starting to sound like Prudence at times, he mused sourly. "Right now I'm looking forward to Hammer Jones," he growled.

Thomas broke off a shrewd appraisal of him. "I reckon that's probably best for the time being," he allowed. "What say we head back to the gym and put in a few rounds of sparring to get you in shape for the Hammer?"

Stark welcomed the chance. Sload seemed to have disappeared, he noted as they entered the gym.

He and Thomas donned gloves. There was no point in risking their hands in a sparring session. As expected, Thomas proved a tough and capable opponent. Stark used footwork to avoid a slugfest, stabbing with his left and counterpunching as Thomas pursued him with the kind of powerful hooking blows that had broken his opponent that Saturday night in the ring. When his fists landed, even on Stark's shoulders and arms, they hurt.

After a spell Thomas drew back and lowered his gloves. Sweat gleamed on his face. "Glad I ain't facing you for real," he commented with a grin. "Ain't never seen a fellow move his feet and punch quite like that. Where'd you pick it up?"

Stark had learned the English style of fisticuffs as part of his mastery of savate, which combined fists and foot fighting. And, with the Pinkertons, he'd studied the new scientific boxing style developed by the European champion, Jem Mace, known as the Swaffham Gypsy. Gentleman Jim Corbett had further perfected the scientific techniques. Finally, for Stark, there'd been that most brutal of schools outside of any ring where the loser wasn't counted out; he was buried.

"Here and there," he answered Thomas's query.

The fighter snorted and raised his gloves before coming warily in again.

Stark was drying off with a towel when he spotted Sload angling through the gloomy gym in his direction. The gambler saw he'd caught Stark's attention and came to a sharp halt. He jerked his head imperiously for Stark to join him. His fleshy lips were drawn thin, and his nostrils were flaring in his pudgy face.

Stark sauntered over, both hands tugging on the towel he'd draped around the back of his neck. If

Sload was looking for trouble, he figured he could pop him in the eyes with the towel before the gambler got a sneak gun into play. He sensed Thomas's curious gaze, but the fighter kept his distance.

"Did you know Bat Masterson is in Guthrie?" Sload demanded without preamble.

How much did Sload know? And why was he hot and bothered about it?

"Yep," Stark told him. He kept his tone careless. "Ran into him a few days ago. He and I go back a spell."

Sload didn't press him for details. "What's he doing here?"

So he didn't know anything for certain, Stark calculated.

He just had ants in his boots from fretting about why the former lawman was in these parts.

It was a danger they should've foreseen, Stark realized grimly. Bat's presence was bound to make the corrupt fight promoters jumpy. Stark needed to do what he could to remedy the problem.

"He said he was here checking into the action at the tables. He gave up being a lawdog, if that's what's got your back up. He's mostly a gambler now; works the tables and anything else that offers a good return on a wager."

"Does that include prizefights?"

Stark hitched his shoulders. "It could. He's been involved before. He was the referee at the Claw-

Hands fight in Wyoming, and the championship bout when Sullivan lost to Kilrain. Then I hear he's cut himself a piece of the action up in Denver doing some promoting."

"You seem to know a mighty lot about him." Sload's eyes were squinted suspiciously.

"No more than any other hombre who follows the fight game, yourself included." Stark sneered. "And don't go getting on your high horse with me. Savvy?"

"Yeah, sure. I just don't cotton to him hanging around these parts. Makes me nervous."

"Afraid he'll cut in on your action?" Stark jeered. "If you want, I'll look him up and ask him what he's doing here."

For a moment Stark hoped he'd hit on a method of contacting Masterson without arousing suspicion.

Then Sload shook his head firmly. "No. The less contact we have with a tinhorn like Masterson, the better off we are. You ride clear of him."

It beat all to hear Sload calling Bat a tinhorn. "Have you started taking odds on me and the Hammer?" Stark asked to get Sload off the subject.

"Too early. We're just getting the word out. By tomorrow or the day after, the marks will be looking to put their money down. But there's already a lot of interest. Seems folks are eager to see the high-and-mighty Peacemaker trying to make peace without using his six-gun or that repeating shotgun.

Some of them who've seen you in action say Jones will have his hands full." Sload's grin was oily and wicked. "But most everybody wants to see the Hammer pound you into the ground like a nail into wood."

"Just like I told you," Stark reminded. His own grin was cold. "You tell them it's the Hammer who's going to get pounded. All that will be left of him is a dent in the wood. Tell him that, too. It ought to stir things up."

"That a fact." Sload shook his head grudgingly. "I got to admit you seem to know what you're doing in this business."

Stark had succeeded in diverting Sload's thoughts from Masterson. He hoped Bat and Nix were canny enough to see the potential danger bred by Bat's presence and take some steps of their own to allay suspicion.

Aloud he asked, "Who are you betting on Saturday night, Sload?"

Sload grinned his evil grin. "I only bet on sure things."

Which, Stark reflected, didn't really answer the question at all.

Chapter Six

"Ladies and gentlemen, in this corner is a man who is a living legend. A gunman extraordinaire, a master gunfighter. Even he has lost track of the men who have gone down beneath his smoking weapon. But tonight he puts aside that infamous Colt six-shooter and faces the most savage fight of his life with only bare knuckles, with which he is also known to be an expert!"

Brother, Stark thought. The announcer should've been a barker at a carney sideshow. But maybe there wasn't that much difference.

The introduction was met with more boos and catcalls than cheers, but the crowd still lifted a hefty racket to the ceiling of the barn.

On his stool across the ring Hammer Jones lived

up to Thomas's description. A thick layer of suet covered his massive muscles. The flab would only make him that much more impervious to blows. A longhorn mustache bristled beneath deepset eyes and a shining bald dome of a skull. His fists seemed big enough to fill gallon buckets. He looked more suited to tangling with grizzly bears than humans.

The seedy announcer launched into the second half of the introductions. It was even longer and more flowery. To hear him tell it, Samson and Hercules had been mere striplings compared to the Hammer.

Like the sudden birth of a mountain out on the prairie, Jones surged to his feet to accept the accolades of the crowd. He snarled at Stark while pumping one fist in the air.

Stark ran his eyes over the crowd. The barn was packed to the rafters. News of the fight had brought everybody and his cousin down from the hills, it seemed. Suddenly Stark squinted through the haze of dust and smoke. For an instant he forgot all about Hammer Jones and the referee and fighting fist and boot.

A familiar dapper figure, complete with derby hat and gold-headed cane, had appeared, accompanied by an even more familiar figure. This one was petite and curved and eye-catching even in such a raucous den of thieves. What in blazes was Bat Masterson doing escorting Prudence McKay here tonight of all nights?

Stark shook his head in disbelief. He fancied he saw Prudence look in his direction, then lift her head to speak to her companion. Bat chuckled, then appeared to gaze in his direction as well.

Then the referee's shouted orders penetrated his hearing, and Thomas's urging propelled him to the center of the ring. He had one last glimpse of the pair. Prudence had her hand resting demurely on Masterson's crooked arm. The next moment Stark's view was cut off by the slab-shouldered bulk of Hammer Jones.

The referee was a sorry-looking yahoo who seemed half drunk. He made mumbled warnings about fouls and gave even more indistinct instructions. Hammer bared his teeth at Stark, and roared from his cavernous mouth.

Stark went back to his corner.

"What's the matter? You moonstruck?" Thomas asked urgently. "Pay attention or you'll get yourself knocked plumb out of the ring before you ever throw a punch!"

The bell rang. Stark went forward to toe the line with the towering form of Hammer Jones.

He had to do three things. First, he had to win. Second, if he wanted to get a chance to fight fist and boot, and be in shape to do it, he had to win fast. The longest bare-knuckle fight on record, be-

tween Andy Bowen and Jack Burke in New Or-
leans, had ended in a draw after one hundred and
ten rounds lasting seven hours. Two nameless sailors reputedly had fought nearly as long in a Chinese
café in St. John's, Newfoundland. Even if he could
survive it, Stark couldn't afford to get bogged down
in such a debilitating ordeal.

Third, and not least, he had to look good if he
wanted folks to keep paying money to see him fight.

None of these three chores looked to be easy to
manage.

With the crowd growling like a hungry beast,
Jones came forward. He hunched his massive shoulders and curved his arms out in front of him, his
hands open.

Jones meant to wrestle, Stark realized, to use his
size and strength to maul his smaller foe into sub-
mission. Stark didn't discount the possiblity. Owen
Swift, the great British featherweight, had suffered
one of his few defeats at the hands of another Hammer, Hammer Lane, who had refused to box. Instead the giant fighter had adopted the tactic of
repeatedly picking up his smaller opponent and
slamming him to the ground. Stark didn't plan to
let this Hammer repeat the performance.

He saw the wicked pleasure in Hammer's eyes as
he moved into the giant's grasp. Then the pleasure
twisted into shock as Stark's straight left jab
smacked him in the face. Stark pivoted to the out-

side, fending off Hammer's reaching arm, and banged at his head with both hands before skipping clear.

Hammer snorted, blew through his nose like a bull, and came after him. Stark turned it into a game of tag, pistoning the left jab—which Jim Corbett had perfected, if not invented—to keep the bald head rocking and swiveling on the thick neck. When Hammer's hands at last lifted to protect his face, Stark squatted low and came in at his body. Right and left, even harder than he'd hit the bag in the gym, he socked his fists into Hammer's gut. The flesh seemed to absorb the blows like soft clay.

Too late Stark glimpsed movement above him. Too late he remembered how Jones had gotten his nickname, and understood that all of the efforts to wrestle him might've been no more than a sham to lure him into exactly this vulnerable spot. The flesh-and-bone mallet of Hammer's fist came crashing down upon him. It glanced off his skull as he tried to jerk clear, then hit his shoulder like a railroad sledge striking a spike.

For a clock-tick the world went black. Then the impact of his knees on the hard floor of the ring jerked him partly back to awareness. A bit by instinct, but just as much by plain weakness, he sagged aside as Jones tried to mash his face with a brutally uplifted knee. It was a clear foul, and if it had landed it might've killed him.

Somewhere the bell was ringing. Round One was over; he'd lost.

He felt the strong hands of Thomas helping him back to his corner. Water splashed in his face, and firm fingers massaged his bruised shoulder.

"You got to watch that hammer blow, Jim," Thomas was chiding him.

Stark growled deep in his throat and straightened on his stool. Jones hadn't even bothered to go back to his corner. He was strutting about the ring to the thunderous approval of the crowd.

Stark drew in air through his nostrils, taking deep breaths, exhaling through his mouth. He shrugged off Thomas's ministrations and snapped up to his feet.

"You still got time!" Thomas exclaimed.

"I don't need it." Stark strode back out into the ring.

Another sound rose from the crowd: murmurs and gasps of shock with maybe just a little grudging respect.

Stark toed the imaginary line dividing the ring in half, and waited for Hammer to take his place facing him. They were glaring eye-to-eye when the bell rang.

Stark almost hurled a roundhouse kick at Hammer. He caught himself in time—no kicking allowed. He missed the foot techniques of savate.

Hammer's clenched fist lifted like a sledge, and

Stark drove his left into the exposed armpit, seeking the nerves buried there. He found them. Hammer's arm sagged. Stark whaled away at his body, ducked and pivoted clear of his reach. Snarling, Jones pursued him. Stark backpedaled, jabbing, then circled to keep from being forced onto the ropes.

As he jabbed again, Hammer ducked his bald head to take the shot on his shaven crown. A good way for a man to bust his knuckles, Stark knew. Old dents like dimples on Hammer's skull showed he'd used the tactic before. He looked up long enough to grin, then lowered his head and bulled forward.

Stark set his feet and uppercut, right and left, one punch hard in the wake of the other. He had all the lift of his shoulders behind the blows, his body swiveling at the waist. His head down, expecting the triphammer jab, Hammer was snapped erect as if he'd been lassoed from behind. Rocking on his heels, he seemed almost ready to topple on over backward. Then he tilted forward solidly onto his feet.

His chin made an easy target, but Stark ignored it. He thrust his right fist full into the exposed throat beneath. Jones choked, gasped, then bent low and lunged, driving his skull up at Stark's jaw in a brutal head butt: a Liverpool kiss.

It was another foul, but the referee didn't seem to be much of a factor in this fight, Stark thought

as he leaned back to get clear. Hammer's gleaming
skull missed him, but the big man's body collided
with his like a runaway horse.

The air was torn from Stark's lungs as he was
driven backward. Then Hammer's thick arms had
locked about him like a couple of boa constrictors,
wrenched him off his feet, and lifted him in the air.

Sweat coursed down their straining bodies. Stark
had the sensation he was being cut in half, but two
could play at fouls. He gouged his elbow beneath
Hammer's chin and into the same spot where his
earlier punch had landed. Hammer's mouth opened
in a great cavity, and his face, inches below that of
Stark, bore the stamp of a barbarian in full battle
rage.

Stark spread his fists wide and drove them simultaneously against Hammer's head. The boa constrictors seemed to go suddenly lax and slither
away. Stark caught his balance as he dropped from
their grip.

Jones collapsed to his knees in front of him. He
was still striving for breath, and his eyes were blank
from the double impact of Stark's fists. But even
then he groped clumsily for his opponent. Stark
backstepped into the clear as the bell rang to end
the round.

Even up.

"You should've hit him an extra lick!" Thomas

advised excitedly in the corner. "I seen you thinking of it."

Stark tended to agree, but he was still glad he'd held back. Mainly, he understood, because Prudence was in the audience. He cast his gaze about but couldn't spot her in the seething mass of spectators.

"The Hammer's headed back to his corner!" Thomas reported as he wiped at Stark's face with a damp cloth.

Stark wasn't surprised. Jones wouldn't be put down for the count that easily. A couple of attendants huddled in front of the big fighter, momentarily blocking him from Stark's view.

Stark took a pull of tepid water and washed it around in his mouth before swallowing. He was on his feet when the bell rang.

Once more they toed the line. Hammer's eyes were partly dazed. And partly crazy. His grin had an unnerving arrogance behind it. At the the referee's signal he lifted his fists in a prizefighting stance.

So the sorry bruiser was finally willing to have a go at fisticuffs, Stark thought with a wicked pleasure. He flicked out a left, then pivoted and threw his right against one of Hammer's battered ears. Jones pivoted himself and swung a lethal right that whistled past Stark's chin as he tilted his head back. In its wake Stark felt a searing touch in his eyes and nostrils.

Iodine! He recognized the scent instantly. Hammer had doused his hands with the stuff. If he managed to rub it into Stark's eyes in a clinch then the fight would be over. Blinded, Stark wouldn't have a chance.

This treacherous lout was full of all kinds of low-down tricks, Stark thought bitterly, and he'd had his fill of it.

Hammer's right fist was back in the classic position. Stark punched—a wicked snaky left—not at the jaw or the body, but under the meaty bicep of Hammer's bent right arm. Hammer gasped as the unexpected blow smacked home. For a heartbeat his arm went limp.

Like he was grabbing a snake by the throat, Stark's hands shot out and clamped on Hammer's weakened limb at wrist and elbow. With his whole lunging body behind the effort, Stark put Hammer's own fist back into his face and dragged the knuckles down across his eyes.

Hammer's hooking left lost power and bounced harmlessly off Stark's shoulder. Jones flung his head back and howled at the heavens. Both hands went up to paw frantically at his eyes—a blinded Cyclops at the mercy of a vengeful Odysseus.

Choosing his spots with care, Stark belabored him with both fists. He couldn't afford to let Jones recover. He didn't cotton to giving the big man another chance to trot out some other foul tactic.

It was no one blow that did it. Stark cut Jones down like a lumberjack going after an oak tree, while the fickle crowd roared its approval. At last Stark set himself and unleashed a final right that was so hard he himself rebounded from the impact.

Jones turned in a slow pivot. Stark caught his balance and stood, fist cocked as the big man crashed down and lay still. He wouldn't be getting up in any thirty seconds, or sixty, for that matter.

Jones had barely been counted out when Thomas hustled Stark from the ring. He shepherded him through the tumult of push and shove and hearty congratulations from well-wishers and gambling winners. Most of the savvy crowd had caught on to what had happened in the final round, the evil iodine gambit.

Unexpectedly Bat Masterson and Prudence appeared, the press of people parting before the magnetism they seemed to generate. Stark caught Thomas's arm before he could block the pair.

"Good fight, Stark." Masterson gripped his shoulder. He was talking loud enough to be heard over the ruckus. He didn't seem to care if Thomas was listening. "Come see me tomorrow. I've a notion we can do business." Prudence glowered at his words.

"I'm willing to listen," Stark played along. What scheme was Masterson hatching?

Stark glanced at Prudence. She sniffed disdainfully, then turned to her escort. "I'll not be a party to you becoming involved in this ugly enterprise, Mr. Masterson!" she declared. "I was under the impression we had come here to observe, not for you to make sordid business deals."

She burned Stark with a glare, then to his amazement graced him with a wink that was no more than the flicker of an eyelash. "I'm waiting, Mr. Masterson."

Masterson grimaced. "I'll expect you tomorrow," he addressed Stark.

"Keno."

Prudence was already drawing him away. They should've both been on stage with that performance, Stark thought. And whatever they were planning, Thomas, no doubt by design, had gotten an earful.

And, no doubt, it would get back to Sload before the night was over.

Chapter Seven

"How's Prudence?" Stark demanded as Masterson opened the door in response to his knock. The words had escaped him before he realized it.

Bat arched an inquiring eyebrow as he ushered Stark into his suite of rooms at the Royal. "The lady is doing quite well, although she's nervous as a cat in a dog pen because she's worried about you. She insisted on accompanying me to the fight. For someone vehemently opposed to the sport, she was certainly excited over your victory." He offered whiskey from a decanter at the room's bar. Stark waved it aside. "The girl has grit," Masterson opined as he sipped his own drink. "I'd say she's a keeper."

"She ain't mine to keep," Stark growled as he

dropped into an easy chair. "It'd be like trying to cozy up to a porcupine."

Masterson didn't answer, just gazed at him steadily over his drink. Stark knew the older man was hitched to Emma, a former burlesque dancer. Their union had lasted some years now. The couple resided in Denver. But, he reminded himself, Masterson had, for the most part, hung up his guns. Even if he dared to think of Prudence along such lines, was he ready to surrender to a civilized life?

Not yet.

"What kind of scheme have you cooked up?" he asked gruffly.

Bat stayed on his feet. He swapped his glass for a cigar from a humidor beside the decanter. Puffing it, he prowled about the room.

"People were starting to talk," he began. "Questions were were being asked about what business I had here. It was making things awkward."

"Sload had some worries about you," Stark advised. "I put him off."

Bat nodded. "Nix and I got our heads together, but it was your Miss McKay who came up with a solution."

"She's not my—never mind," Stark dropped his protest. "I'll bet I can guess her idea: you're fixing to buy into the fight game."

"Let's say for now, I'm investigating the possibility. That way I can keep an eye on you. Prudence was very concerned over our inability to keep track of your whereabouts and well-being."

"Is that a fact?" Stark murmured.

"She proposed that once you had established yourself in the good graces of the Yanger brothers, I step in as your manager and promoter. I went her one further."

"How's that?"

Masterson halted his pacing and grinned coldly. "You and I take over the whole operation. Then the Eastern syndicate bosses have to come to us. When they do, we nail their hides to the wall."

"Taking over might not be easy. The Yanger boys have a passel of hired guns backing them."

"Two-bit gun throwers," Bat dismissed them with contempt. "You think for one minute they'll be willing to go up against Bat Masterson and the Peacemaker? They'll collapse like a house of cards."

Stark knew what it was to have a reputation and a fast gun. But Bat Masterson had been a name to conjure with in the hard-bitten towns and cities of the West for going on two decades now. His presence alone had been enough to quiet more than one ornery cowtown in his lawman days. Stark recalled the tale of Masterson and Tilghman laying out the streets of Guthrie.

He grinned at the older man, a tingle of excitement riding him. "Us against the Yanger guns? I reckon those are odds I'd take."

Nope, he wasn't ready to hang it up just yet.

After he left Masterson, he headed for the gym. He carried some aches and pains from the mauling Jones had given him, and some shadowboxing wouldn't hurt him any. Jones had just been a warm-up, he reminded himself.

He accepted the congratulations from some of the fighters and hangers-on at the gym. He ignored the scowls of those who'd lost money on Jones, or who just plain didn't cotton to him taking a hand in the fight game. There were quite a few of the latter, but watching his back had long ago become an acquired reflex with him.

He found a jar of grease and applied it thoroughly to his hands. He couldn't afford to let this job hamper his ability to handle a six-shooter in the future.

Provided he survived fighting fist and boot.

He was moving his feet, throwing a few tentative punches at thin air when he spotted the stout shape of Sload headed determinedly in his direction. Trailing him not quite so eagerly was Thomas's husky figure. Stark grinned thinly. He had a notion what was coming, but he had a few things to get off his chest first.

As Sload drew near, Stark turned smoothly and darted out a jab that made Sload pull up sharply to keep from running into it. "I got a bone to pick with you, mister," Stark grated.

The promoter's determination faltered. "Listen,"

he began defensively, "if it's about the iodine and the rest of the fouls—"

"You're blamed right it's about the fouls," Stark cut him off. He jabbed again, close enough that Sload flinched. "I didn't sign onto this misbegotten outfit to let a big ox like Jones cripple me or blind me, because he's got a different set of rules!"

"None of that was my doing!" Sweat shone on Sload's brow. "Jones and his cronies cooked that up, and he'll pay for it!"

"If it happens again, you'll be the one doing the paying," Stark vowed. He didn't know if he'd gotten the straight goods or not, but he didn't much care. The role he was playing called for a harsh reaction to Hammer's tactics. "Now," he went on, easing up a little, "what's eating you?"

Sload squared his shoulders. "Word is, you had dealings with Bat Masterson since the fight. I, that is, the Yanger brothers want to know what the two of you talked about."

"He made me a proposition, and I turned him down," Stark answered flatly. "Anything else bothering you?"

"What kind of proposition?"

Stark stared at him until Sload's bulging eyes shifted away. "He wanted to back me," Stark replied then. "But he wanted too big of a slice of my winnings, and there's nothing that says he'd do me any good at getting to fight fist and boot. Relax, Sload.

Your deal with me is safe, so long as you don't start dealing off the bottom. I still have the suspicion that's what you did on that fight last night."

Sload wagged his head back and forth. "I told you, you've got that wrong. Jones didn't fancy being ordered to fight you, when he was looking to fight fist and boot style again. He wasn't going to let you win and knock him out of the contention for fist and boot."

It made a certain amount of sense, and Stark let the matter drop. It had served its purpose. He hoped his fight with Jones had done the same.

"When do I meet with your bosses?" he demanded.

"We ride out tomorrow," Sload told him. "Thomas, you're coming along."

"Yessir."

"Where are we riding?" Stark pressed.

"You'll know when we get there. In the meantime, don't let anything happen to you; you're cash on the hoof from here on out. Thomas, take care of him."

"I don't need a keeper," Stark advised coldly.

"Like I just said, you're worth money now. I'm looking after an investment." Sload turned dismissively away from Stark. "Thomas, you've done good work. I'll see that something gets set up for you on the next fight night."

"Thank you, Mr. Sload."

Sload ambled off. Stark glanced expressionlessly at Thomas.

"I wasn't looking to interfere with your business, Mr. Stark," he offered hurriedly. "But I had to report that you were going to have a confab with Masterson."

Stark hitched his shoulders in a shrug. "Forget it; you were just doing your job."

The stocky fighter grinned with relief. "Mighty glad you see it that way."

How far could he trust the man? Stark wondered. For now, Thomas was a good source of information, and he knew his way around. But the time would likely come when he'd get crossways with Stark's job. Was he a possible ally? The lure of big winnings had drawn him into the illicit fight trade. But Stark sensed an uneasiness in him at the notion of two men fighting no holds barred for the pleasure of bloodthirsty spectators.

For a lot of reasons, he needed to keep an eye on Thomas.

When they headed out the next morning, Stark kept an eye not only on the fighter, but on Sload and his two gun-hung bodyguards as well. Riding beside the promoter's carriage, they bore the stamp of the sorry breed of fighting men the Yanger brothers were reputed to have hired. Stark suspected they might be part of that private army. At any rate, it made good sense to have gun-savvy hombres siding you when you crossed the boundary known as Hell's Fringe and entered into the Indian lands.

As U.S. Marshal, Evett Nix and his deputies shared a limited jurisdiction with the police of several of the tribes which had been forcibly located here to this vast expanse of grassland and wilderness. But in real terms the law in Indian Territory was whatever the fastest gun made it.

Known all over the country and beyond as a haven for wanted men, cutthroats, and bandits, the Indian lands were a bastion of lawlessness. Outlaw gangs such as the Daltons leased pastureland from various of the tribes and holed up there between raids into Oklahoma Territory, or robberies of trains crossing through the Lands. Lawmen and posses rode into the teeth of danger once they crossed the boundary.

If the Yanger boys wanted to stage gladiator fights, this was the place to do it, Stark reflected bleakly.

He was astride Red, his big sorrel stallion. The horse was happy to be out on the range again after his sojurn in one of Guthrie's stables. There was an eagerness to his gait that kept Stark busy at reining him in.

Stark knew how the beast felt. It was good to be making some headway at last. He was armed for bear, just like always when he traveled these regions. His handguns and bowie knife rode in their usual places. Sheathed on his saddle, one on either side, were his lever-action long guns: a Winchester ten-gauge repeating shotgun, and a high-caliber 1886 Winchester sporting rifle. Bandoliers of ammo criscrossed his chest.

Sload's eyes had widened when he laid them on the armament. "You fixing to fight a war?" he asked caustically.

"Only if one comes along," Stark answered. "You got any objections?"

Sload didn't. And the two hired guns kept a wary distance as the party traveled.

Stark glanced at Thomas riding beside him. They had fallen back behind the buggy. The fighter forked a serviceable gray gelding. From the familiar ease with which he sat the saddle, Thomas must've spent some time in his career as a cowboy.

"Looks like you've punched cows in your day," Stark put the thought into words.

Thomas grinned. "That and just about every other hard-luck job you can think of. I've swamped floors, cleaned a livery, even was a bouncer in a gambling hall for a spell."

"How'd you get into prizefighting?"

"I was never one to crawfish from a scrap, and I had my share of back-alley brawls as a kid. I won't stand for no man insulting me. Well, one day a carnival came to town, and they had a fellow who'd take on all comers in the ring. Since I'd been fighting for free, I thought I may as well try it for money. When I whipped that old boy and won the prize, the carney owner up and hired me."

"Hard way to make a living," Stark commented.

Thomas sobered some. "Truth is, I don't like hurting folks. But if a man's willing to fight me for pay, I'll sure enough oblige him."

Stark nodded at the old revolver riding carelessly in a battered slip-on holster. "Ever have much occasion to use that?"

"A few times. Never killed nobody with it. Heaven forbid that I should. I ain't looking to kill no one."

"Not even with your fists?" Stark prodded. "I thought that was the point of fighting fist and boot."

"Some folks see it that way," Thomas allowed. "But when I'm in the ring, or if I'm fighting outside of it, my aim is to beat the other man, not to kill him. I've won a lot more fights than I've lost, and I've never killed a man."

Stark could barely remember what it was like to have never killed a man.

Something must've showed in his face because Thomas squared his shoulders and spoke up. "I hear you've done plenty of killing with all them weapons you're packing, maybe with your hands, for all I know. Still, you don't strike me as an hombre who enjoys it, like some I've seen."

Stark could've talked about fighting the good

fight with guns instead of fists. But, he recalled in time, Thomas was a part of what he was trying to destroy. He might even end up being another victim for him to remember.

Heaven forbid.

"A man does what he's called to," Stark said aloud.

Chapter Eight

A spattering of shots sounded from over the ridge ahead, and Sload pulled his buggy to a halt. He glanced at one of the mounted gunsels. "Go check it out."

The fellow cantered off obediently. Carelessly he skylined himself as he crested the ridge. Stark's mouth curled in disgust.

"The Bar Y is just over yonder," Sload explained. "Probably nothing but some of the boys letting off steam. Still, it doesn't hurt to be careful."

Stark agreed on both counts. Amidst the shots had been the drum roll of a six-shooter being fanned. For the stunt to be effective in a showdown, the gun had to be specially altered, and the target not much more than five feet in front of the barrel.

Most seasoned pros wouldn't rely on such a trick on a bet. But a lot of greenhorns practiced it endlessly. Most of them never lived to become seasoned pros. The careless guard probably wouldn't either.

They had ridden through half the morning of the second day. The countryside was made up of the same rolling grassland. They had seen only a few other mounted travelers. Just one group—a pack of down-at-the-heels brigands—had ventured close, probably expecting a party with a buggy would be easy prey. A good look at the riders accompanying the conveyance had changed their minds in a hurry.

The scout came loping back from his mission. "All clear," he reported, hauling up cruelly on his mount. "Just a little target practice going on."

Sload nodded and jigged his team forward. The party topped the ridge. Before them, on a level stretch of prairie, flanked by the wooded course of a creek, lay the Yanger homestead.

The headquarters of the Bar Y, Stark noted, bore little sign of being a working ranch. There was a two-story house, a barn with an empty corral, and a scattering of outbuildings, one of them a bunkhouse.

Horses grazed on lush pastureland beyond the corral, and at least a dozen men lounged about the premises. A handful of them were engaged in shooting it out with tin cans set on the middle rail of the

corral. None of the sharpshooters seemed to care
that the horses might be at risk from stray bullets.
There wasn't a trace of a legitimate cowboy.

The outfit was more like a barracks for an undis-
ciplined army than it was a ranch, Stark mused. The
brothers must be pretty sure of themselves to let
their security be this lax. But, according to the talk,
none of the illicit fights took place on these premises anyway.

An aged hostler with a stove-up leg emerged
from the barn to see to their horses as they reached
the house. The two bodyguards, their duty apparently done, drifted off toward the site of the target
practice.

Sload looked over at Thomas. "Scram," he ordered. "I'll holler when you're needed."

The fighter's features flushed even darker. He
nodded curtly and strode away.

Sload wasn't through throwing orders around.
"Wait here, Stark."

"Shake a leg," Stark tossed out an order of his
own. "I didn't ride this far to sit around while you
palaver with the big boys all by your lonesome."

"Don't worry, I'm looking after our interests,"
Sload assured him.

"In maybe five minutes I'll be in to look after my
own," Stark promised.

Grunting with effort, Sload mounted the steps

onto the wide wraparound porch. He disappeared into the house.

Stark looked about. Truth be told, he didn't mind the wait. It gave him a chance to size up the ranch headquarters a little better.

He realized one of the buildings was actually a sort of depot for a spur of railroad track that ended with a turnaround here at the Bar Y. The tales of high rollers being hauled here on private Pullmans must be true.

A couple of the loafing hardcases meandered over. Their eyes widened a little as they took in the armament adorning him.

"I go by Chad," the taller one said by way of introduction. "You got business here?" He was lanky to the point of gauntness.

Stark took his time about answering. "Looks that way, don't it?" he drawled.

The smaller one—a weasel with a gun—snorted and hitched his shoulders. "You got a handle?"

"Yep."

"Well, let's have it, pronto!"

Stark used his left forefinger to tilt the brim of his Stetson back a hair. "Stark."

That shook them a little bit as it sank in.

"You the hombre they call the Peacemaker?" Chad asked.

"Been called all kinds of things. Including that."

The pair exchanged sidelong glances, which was

a fool thing when facing a possible foe loaded down with more guns than both of them were packing put together.

"You coming aboard to ramrod us?" Chad asked with an edge of hostility.

He must hold that position right now, Stark thought. There was no need of getting crosswise of him.

Yet.

"Hoping to make some money in the ring," he advised.

"Is that a fact?" the short one blurted. "Who you fixing to fight?"

"Top dog, whoever that is. Not much point in fighting otherwise."

The short gunman vented a shrill whistle through his gaping teeth. "Shoot! The Peacemaker fixing to go up against Blake Gar! That'll sure enough be something to see."

"He's pretty rough, huh?" Stark probed.

"Mean and dirty is more like it. He's killed or crippled the last five men he's fought."

"How's he done that?"

The hardcase shook his head. "I've seen him do it, and I couldn't rightly tell you. Seems like something different every time. He's so fast it's hard to follow. His fights sure don't last long, but the crowd always loves to see him bring the other fellow down in jig time."

"So he's the champ at fighting fist and boot, huh?"

"That's a fact. So far nobody's beat him."

Stark chewed it over. A hunch nudged him. He made to ask another question, but Sload's voice interrupted.

"Come on, Stark." The promoter stood on the porch. "They'll see you."

Stark gave the pair of gunhands a companionable nod, then followed Sload's heavy, slouching form inside.

The house was high dollar; give the Yanger boys that, Stark thought. Indian rugs, upholstered furniture, a cavernous fireplace, and mounted heads of dead animals cluttered a huge living area. A bar—nicer than those in any but the best saloons—ran the full length of one wall. An attractive woman in an expensive gown apparently served as bartender. She watched as they passed. Her pale face was as expressionless as carved ivory.

Sload led Stark past the doorway to a lavish dining room where visiting high rollers were no doubt wined and dined. Further along the hall a glass-fronted gun case displayed a nice collection of long guns. In addition to a good selection of lever-actions of various makes, there was an old Sharps Big Fifty and a heavy-caliber Mannlicher. All looked to be well-oiled and ready for use.

Two men were in the plush office Stark entered

in Sload's wake. One was seated behind a cluttered acre-sized desk, while the other prowled as restlessly as a hungry catamount.

The Yanger brothers shared the same sort of broad features that would draw a lot of women to them. Clint, the eldest, was showing gray in the light brown of his hair. He was the businessman of the two, Stark recalled. He seemed to relish the role as he lounged behind his deak. He had even adopted a fancy lawyer's suit, complete with vest and tie. The coat hung from a coat tree. The vest strained beneath a bulging midriff that said he probably hadn't dirtied his manicured hands with any type of physical labor or range work in a good long spell.

Burt was the gunhawk who had a handful of notches to his credit. Lean and surly, he might almost have passed for one of the gunsels on payroll, except his pearl-handled pistol and tooled gun belt were too expensive for any dollar-a-dozen hired gun. Then, too, his yellow eyes carried the baleful contented gleam of a gunman who doesn't have to pull his weapon for wages. He pulled it for pleasure, and from the hungry look of him, he was eager to taste powder smoke again.

Clint leaned back in his leather-upholstered swivel chair. His desk held a mess of papers, coffee cups, bottles, and other debris, including an over-under derringer.

"Sload's been telling us all about you, Stark,"

Clint began without preliminary. "He's nearly got us convinced that everybody concerned could make a little money if you climbed into our ring."

"More than a little," Stark declared flatly. "People will pay a lot to see me fight your champion. And they'll bet even more over whether or not I'll win or walk out alive."

Clint's gaze was speculative, like he was judging a prime head of beef. In his mind, he likely was. "You figure you can win?"

"From what I hear, I'm betting my life on it."

"Tell us why you suddenly got interested in fighting fist and boot."

Once more he had to do some convincing, Stark thought. And this time it was for all the marbles.

Burt stopped his prowling and halted behind and a little to one side of his brother. He stood with hands clasped loosely in front of him. Gunfighter's stance—he could draw from there with a flick of his hand.

"I make my living fighting," Stark said. "And I demand and get top dollar for my services. Guns, knives, fists, it makes no difference. Maybe I'm best known for my gun work, but those kind of jobs are drying up lately. Things are getting civilized even out here." It was easy for him to add a twist of bitterness to his words. "I go where the money is, and I go where the fighting is. Right now, they're both here."

Clint extracted a cigar from somewhere under the rubble on his desk. He bit off the tip like a barroom brawler going after an opponent's finger, and spat it carelessly back onto the desk. He clamped the cigar unlit between square yellowed teeth.

"I always heard you're a straight shooter when it comes to picking jobs, nothing to get you crossways with the law," he remarked skeptically.

"I won't backshoot an innocent man, if that's what you're getting at. But from what I hear there's not going to be much shooting in the ring, unless there's even fewer rules than I've been told."

Behind his brother, Burt let out a harsh chuckle. "Oh, there's rules: No excessive biting or gouging. And if there's too much wrestling or ducking each other, or dancing so it ain't interesting to the crowd, we have a couple of gents standing by with black-snakes to liven things up."

Referees armed with bullwhips to goad reluctant fighters, Stark thought sourly. That was a pretty good symbol for this barbaric enterprise.

"So your motives are pure as gold," Clint summarized. "I reckon I can appreciate that." He finally got around to setting fire to his cigar, and puffed hard on it as he stood up. "Let's all of us get a little more comfortable and discuss this like gentlemen."

He led the way back into the large living area. Burt paced beside Stark, eyeing him from the edge of his vision. Stark was reminded again of a cougar he'd had occasion to see up close in the wild. The cougar was more trustworthy, he figured.

Clint got them seated in a grouping of fancy leather chairs. The pale woman from the bar glided over to take orders. Sload eyed her lecherously. Stark shook his head when she glanced inquiringly at him. Clint frowned at Stark's refusal.

"I never drink while I'm talking business," Stark told him.

Whiskey glass in one hand and cigar in the other, the elder brother leaned back. He was clearly enjoying this farce of a business meeting. Maybe he pictured himself as chairman of a bank back East.

"Clint and me are orphans from down in Texas," he advised. "We got took in by a fellow who staged prizefights. Most of our schooling was watching bare-knuckle bouts or listening to our foster pa make deals. That's how we learned the ins and outs of the fight game. Sometimes he arranged pretty big bouts. Even had some wealthy backers from New York City involved. He took us up there when we were still lads. Have to say, he showed us a right fine time." Clint's smile at the memories was laced with decadence.

"Sounds like quite an upbringing," Stark commented.

"That it was," Clint agreed. "Anyway, a deal over a fight in Kansas went sour and ended in shooting. Burt here was already packing a gun, and he dropped the fellow who did for our foster pa. That was Burt's first," he added with brotherly pride.

"It's eight now," Burt asserted with a wicked twist of his lips. "All in standup fights, fastest gun wins."

"I heard it was six," Stark remarked mildly.

Burt bristled. "You heard wrong!" He lifted both hands, opening and closing his right like he was clasping the butt of a pistol. Stark saw heavy calluses on the heel of the palm of his left hand.

"My mistake," Stark said aloud. There wasn't any percentage in prodding this would-be gunfighter right now. But Burt just flat rubbed him the wrong way. "How'd you end up here in the Indian lands?" he asked Clint to defuse the younger brother.

Clint flicked a peremptory finger back over his shoulder. Sullenly, Burt subsided.

"Me and Burt carried right on in the fight business," Clint took up where he'd left off. "We already had all the contacts, and I had a better head for business than the old man ever did. Burt handled any trouble that came along." Behind him, Burt grinned tightly at Stark.

"I'd always figured even bare-knuckle fighting was too tame," Clint explained. "There's plenty of folks who want to see more than a dancing exhibition in the ring. They want real fighting, just like back in the Roman days. The gloves they used then had spikes on them. I had a hankering to try setting up something like that, but the do-gooders and the holy joes are making it harder and harder to stage even a bare-knuckle fight these days. The fight business ain't what it used to be. It's a sorry state of affairs when some song and dance with gloves and timed rounds is billed as a fight."

"So you came out to the lands where hardly anything's illegal." Stark led him on. He was getting tired of this seamy family history.

"You hit it right on the button! I got hitched to an Indian gal so's we could have as much land as we wanted. She up and left me finally, complaining I was too mean too her. Good riddance, I say. And I still can lay claim to the land.

"We staged a few bouts and word spread fast. Before long we had rich folks from all over the country coming to see the show. It was easy to get backing from that New York money. I guess you saw the railroad spur we had laid here to accommodate our clientele."

"Just who are these New York backers of yours?"

Clint shook his head with a grin. "I'm not prone to mentioning their names. They don't like publicity, and they're not the sort you'd want to cross."

Stark let it ride. He hadn't figured it'd be that easy. "So when do I fight Gar?"

Clint cocked an eyebrow. "You figure to start right at the top, do you?"

Stark cut a glance at Sload. "That was the deal.

I didn't come all the way out here to fight another Hammer Jones. You set me up with Gar, or the whole shebang's over with."

Burt stirred uneasily at his tone. Stark was watching both of them. Clint was in charge, but Burt was the more dangerous, and Clint might not always be able to keep him on his leash. And too, he hadn't forgotten that derringer within Clint's reach.

"Sload said you drove a hard bargain," Clint mused aloud. "But he also said you'd be worth it. I reckon he was right on both counts. You got a rep as a top professional fighting man. Even I'm kind of interested in seeing what happens when the two of you get together in the ring. Don't disappoint me."

Stark smiled thinly. "Gar's the one who's going to be disappointed."

Burt relaxed, but his sneer was mocking. *Not likely to be rooting for me*, Stark reflected wryly.

"My cut's thirty-five percent," he announced flatly.

Burt bristled up, but Clint stilled him again with a flick of his hand. He chewed on his cigar as he calculated. Clearly Sload had already advised him of Stark's demand. At last he nodded. "Done." He cut off his brother's outraged protest by adding, "That's after expenses, and provided you win. You lose, and if you're still living, you get nothing."

Stark shrugged. "Those are the terms of most of

my jobs." He stood up. "Give me the date and I'll be here."

"Uh-uh, it ain't that easy," Clint drawled. Burt had gone tense again. "We'll need three or four weeks to get the fight set up. Until then you stay at one of our training camps here in the lands."

"I don't cotton to being a prisoner," Stark said coldly, though he wasn't too surprised at the development.

Clint hitched his shoulders. "Nothing personal. We handle all our fist and boot fighters this way before a bout. Just a precaution to keep word from leaking out to the wrong ears. And the training camps aren't as bad as they sound. You'll have anything you want: whiskey, female companionship, gambling." He smiled lecherously, then sobered. "Unless you've got some reason to leave?" His tone was a challenge.

"None in particular," Stark said. "But if I find one, your rules and your hired guns won't stop me."

"If you ride out before the fight, then the deal's off," Clint said flatly. "Your choice."

"For now, I'll choose to stay."

"Don't get uppity with us, Peacemaker!" Burt snarled. The fingers of his gunhand curled. His left hand hovered at his side.

Stark let contempt flare in his eyes. "And you don't go butting heads with the professionals, sonny."

Stark wheeled and strode from the room. He was gambling Clint still held the whiphand over his hot-headed brother. The gamble paid off; no shots were flung at his retreating back.

But he had a lot bigger gamble ahead against Blake Gar.

Chapter Nine

"Two Eastern gentlemen are here to see you, Miss McKay. They do not have appointments, nor will they state their business."

Prudence pulled her attention away from the legal brief she was preparing. Martha, her secretary, was not well-disposed toward her visitors, she noted. The austere widow and former schoolmarm had not worked for her very long. But already she guarded the portals of her employer's office with a fierce and unflinching loyalty.

She had shut the door behind her as she entered, clearly wanting the opportunity to express her opinion of the newcomers.

"Did they give their names?" Prudence asked.

She had come to respect the older woman's judgment.

"A Mr. Arthur Tallant from New York, and his associate, Mr. Lecker."

Prudence felt a nettling at the nape of her neck. New York? What could Eastern businessmen want with her? *If* they were legitimate businessmen . . .

"Very well," she announced. "Give me a minute and then show them in." She would draw her own conclusions about the pair.

Martha sniffed her disapproval and exited the office, closing the door firmly behind her.

Rising, Prudence took her jacket from the coat tree and slipped into it. Waist length, it complemented her matching skirt and modest white blouse. She fluffed her dark curls and automatically checked her appearance in a hand mirror from a desk drawer. As always these days, the routine action made her wonder irrelevantly how she would look in James Stark's eyes. Concern over his welfare these past days since he had seemingly disappeared had only heightened her distraction from her daily office work.

In her heart of hearts she was finding it harder and harder to deny that her feelings toward him were strictly platonic. From the way her pulse quickened when she thought of him, there was no denying it at all.

That last evening with him had been heavenly.

But it had ultimately been marred by their mock quarrel. In her ears it had sounded all too close to real words they had exchanged from time to time in their tumultuous relationship. And she still blushed with mortification and excitement at the memory of the compulsion which had drawn her shamelessly to his suite to bid him farewell. The sight of him bare-chested in the doorway returned to her still at unexpected moments.

But even given the dubious possibility that she and Jim could establish or maintain anything beyond their current nebulous friendship, what would it be like to be married to a man who lived by the gun?

Her heartfelt opposition to violence had yielded at last to acknowledge the need of men of his ilk. But it was bad enough waiting for him and fretting about him now when he was absent. How much worse would it be if they were more than friends? How could she stand having her husband ride off to parts unknown on perilous missions, never knowing when Evett Nix, or a telegram, or some stranger would come bringing news of his final fate?

Abruptly she recalled that Bat Masterson had a wife who must deal with just such circumstances. Maybe she could find an opportunity to ask him. . . .

With a shake of her head that disarrayed her curls a bit, she banished such frivolous notions from her mind. She had possible new clients awaiting, albeit of a rather curious nature.

She was standing behind her desk with her best air of competent assurance when Martha ushered her visitors into the office. As was her custom she rounded the desk to greet them and shake hands. The tactic generally unsettled men and helped them get past the fact of her gender. It also gave her a chance to size up who she was dealing with.

And she had quite a bit of sizing up to do with this pair, she realized immediately. Arthur Tallant was in his thirties, well educated, with appealing good looks that were only enhanced by his easy air of confidence. Oddly though, his eyes were hooded, as if he was concealing his real thoughts behind his mask of cool competence.

"Miss McKay, my pleasure to meet you." If he was put off by shaking hands with her, he certainly didn't show it. His grip was firm and sure. "This is my associate, Mr. Lecker."

If she was having trouble assessing Tallant, she had no such trouble in taking the measure of his colleague. She had been around James Stark, and the separate breed of men with which he dealt, too long to make any mistake about Mr. Lecker. His alert aura of awareness, of tension that never quite eased, of tightly contained power, branded him so clearly that she didn't even need to see the firearm he no doubt carried beneath his tailored coat. He

was a high-dollar hired gun, likely a bodyguard for
Tallant, but at any rate a man who would work either side of the law if the price was right.

"Have a seat, gentlemen." Her intuitive assessment of the man with only a surname, and the possible implications of it, had come in a flash of time.
She let none of it show on her face, nor in her gracious manners.

"Thank you, Miss McKay. I'll accept your offer."
Tallant was easily her match in graciousness. "Mr.
Lecker prefers to stand, if you'll pardon him."

Wordlessly the gunman positioned himself
against the wall near the door. From there he could
survey the entire room, as well as have an edge on
anybody entering with hostile intent. Prudence did
her best to ignore him, but his presence hovered like
a brooding thundercloud. Mr. Tallant must travel in
dangerous circles, Prudence reflected.

"We're certainly enjoying our visit here to your
fine city, Miss McKay." Tallant seemed to feel the
need for some polite small talk before getting down
to business.

"How may I help you?" Prudence felt no such
need.

Tallant's friendliness cooled slightly. "I'm here
acting as agent and attorney-in-face for a principal
with significant business interests in New York and
elsewhere."

"Does he have a name?"

"He prefers that his identity remain confidential at this time."

Prudence accepted the secrecy for the moment. "Go on," she urged.

"My principal has recognized that Oklahoma Territory is burgeoning with possibilities for the shrewd investor. There are many lucrative enterprises available. They will assuredly increase once the Indian lands are opened for settlement and statehood is granted. Cattle, mining, land speculation, and other opportunities are rife here."

"The tribes may not be eager to turn their land over to investors," Prudence observed.

Tallant sneered. "They'll have no choice in the matter when the pressure to open their holdings becomes too great for the government to withstand."

Prudence feared he was correct. It wouldn't be the first time the tribes had lost out, or the last. She dropped the matter. "Does your employer need legal representation?"

Tallant pursed his lips. "Right to the point, aren't you, Miss McKay? I'm beginning to understand how you've earned your reputation."

"I haven't earned it by wasting time."

"As you say," Tallant conceded. "My principal believes that he may, indeed, require competent legal services in the near future. After studying his alternatives he believes you are best suited for the job."

"And just what job is that?"

Tallant sighed. "My employer would like to have you on retainer in anticipation of such time as a need arises for your services. He's willing to be quite generous in these matters."

His answers weren't telling her much. "How generous?" she persisted.

Tallant slipped a supple hand inside his coat and brought out an unmarked and unsealed envelope. His eyes glittered and his smile was somehow wicked as he flicked back the flap and thumbed out a spread fan of currency. "You'll find five hundred dollars here as your first month's retainer. An identical sum will be sent each month. As I said, *quite* generous." He extended the envelope and its contents confidently toward her.

Prudence had the sudden impression she was being asked to accept a gift from the devil himself: Satan offering fruit from the forbidden tree.

But Prudence had learned from Eve's mistake. She kept her hands where they were.

"Your boss is willing to pay me six thousand dollars a year simply to be available in case he has need of legal representation?"

"In effect, yes."

"What do you mean, 'in effect'?"

A bit reluctantly Tallant withdrew the proffered fruit. "As I'm sure you understand, a man in my principal's position must be careful not to inadvertently damage potential business associates or situations."

"I'm sorry," Prudence said demurely. "What does that mean to me?"

"It's our understanding," Tallant began carefully, "that from time to time you have written opinion columns for one of the leading newspapers here."

At last Prudence was sure what this meeting was about. She felt a heightening of her senses, a tautening of her courtroom combat reflexes honed by years of legal battles. But when she spoke, her tone was even and balanced. "I've written two pieces for the editorial page," she confirmed.

The second column denouncing the fight racket had been her own idea, one which Nix and Masterson had approved. It would serve, they hoped, the purpose of further distancing her from Jim, as well as from Masterson in his new role as a well-known sporting man interested in the local action.

The scathing column, she understood now, had had the added result of stirring up some concern among the mysterious New York backers. The courteous Mr. Tallant and his menacing associate were representatives of at least one such backer. Her goal now must be to learn his identity.

"I'm still not sure I understand," she said aloud.

"As a condition of my principal retaining your services, he would like to have, shall we say, an editor's right to approval of future columns prior to publication."

Prudence tilted her head. "That's an odd requirement."

She was in a quandary. If she accepted the outrageous retainer she would arguably be establishing an attorney–client relationship, and binding herself with the client's privilege of confidentiality. Ethically she couldn't take the retainer with the sole intent of learning her client's identity so that she could expose his involvement in illicit activities to the authorities.

"You must understand my employer's position," Tallant pressed on in his best persuasive manner.

He had quite a spiel. Prudence listened to his prevarications and deliberately misleading assertions until he fell silent. His handsome face bore a look of confident expectation.

"I couldn't possibly even consider accepting your principal as a client without first knowing his identity." Prudence's words wiped some of the confidence from his features. She was far more tempted by learning her would-be client's name than she was by the offered money, but ethically she could go no further in attempting to draw it from his agent.

Tallant studied her for a long moment of assessment. What he discerned gave a troubled cast to his features. "I'm truly sorry to hear that, Miss Mc-

Kay," he said resignedly, returning the money to his breast pocket at last.

But still he lingered. Clearly he didn't relish reporting back to his employer without some commitment by her. At length he set his jaw firmly. "May I trust in your discretion if I reveal my employer's identity?"

"You have my solemn promise that I will use my best discretion," Prudence assured with a clear conscience.

"Very well, Miss McKay. I shall trust your discretion. My principal is Benjamin Standard. You may have heard of him." An arrogant pride tinged his voice.

Prudence had indeed heard of the ruthless Eastern tycoon and business magnate. The rumors of powerful backers of the no-holds-barred fights were certainly true.

"I regret," she announced aloud, "that I have conflicts of interest that prevent me from accepting Mr. Standard as a client." Once again she could speak with a clear conscience, she thought thankfully.

She could see that Tallant understood that he had gambled and lost. But he couldn't be sure of her motives, and so he played another hand. "I'm sure Mr. Standard would waive any objections to such matters."

"It would still be ethically impossible for me to represent him," she countered firmly.

Frustration flared in Tallant's shrewd eyes, but he held himself in check. "Just the same, I'll leave this here in case you should reconsider." He produced the envelope almost by sleight of hand and placed it reverently on the table. "Keep it as compensation for your time during this meeting, in any case."

"My rates aren't that high." She left the envelope untouched and met his gaze squarely.

Grudgingly he withdrew the envelope and rose to his feet. "You would do well in the business world, Miss McKay, I believe."

"As well as Mr. Standard?"

He grinned as if the notion was amusing. "Mr. Standard is a power unto himself. He won't be happy that I've failed in my mission." He cocked his head thoughtfully. "But my trip here doesn't need to be a total loss. I would be honored if you would show me around Guthrie this evening, Miss McKay."

Looking at him, Prudence thought that business matters would never be over for him. If she accepted his offer he would use his formidable charm and persuasive skills to attempt to get her to change her mind regarding his employer's offer. She had no doubt he would also attempt to obtain certain other more personal favors from her as well.

"I'm afraid I have prior commitments."

"Then perhaps tomorrow evening."

"No thank you." She rose in dismissal, not offering her hand. "Give my regards to Mr. Standard upon your return to New York."

Tallant stood. Even standing on the other side of her desk, he towered above her. His eyes had gone opaque. If Standard lived up to his reputation of ruthlessness, then his minion probably bid fair to match him, she reflected darkly. Behind Tallant she saw the gunman's lips lift in a faint smirk of satisfaction at Tallant's defeat.

"This way, gentlemen." With consummate timing Martha had appeared in the doorway. She ushered the pair out, casting one brief approving glance over her shoulder before she disappeared.

Tension strummed Prudence's nerves in the aftermath of the meeting. Still, she forced herself to wait until she felt certain her visitors were well clear of the building before leaving her office to make her way to the Harriot Building. She found Evett Nix closeted with a taut Bat Masterson.

"Bat took the risk of coming to see me," Nix said with little preliminary. "He's got news."

"James is set to fight fist and boot three weeks from tomorrow," Masterson told her. "The news is making the rounds of the gaming houses now. I just got word of it myself."

Prudence quashed the sharp thrust of anxiety that seared through her stomach. "What are your plans?" she asked as steadily as she could manage.

"I'll be there. After the fight, James and I will make our move."

Assuming Jim wins, Prudence thought despairingly. *Assuming he lives.*

"I just learned something as well," she announced to cover her discomfiture, and went on to tell of her meeting with the persuasive Mr. Tallant and his associate. Masterson and Nix listened solemnly.

"That's the first real progress we've made," Nix said when she finished. "Congratulations."

"It's still not enough to act on," Prudence cautioned.

Nix nodded. "We need Standard himself present at one of the fights."

"James and I will get him there," Masterson promised.

Or die trying, Prudence added grimly to herself. A vision of the lethal Mr. Lecker flashed in her mind.

"I better not stay around here any longer." Masterson rose, collecting his derby and gold-headed cane.

"Bat, could I speak with you a moment?" Prudence said before she quite realized what she was doing.

"My pleasure, I'm sure." Masterson's eyes were puzzled.

Prudence cast an imploring glance at Nix.

"Feel free to step into the conference room just

through that door there," the marshal offered. He too looked a bit perplexed.

Prudence's face was burning as Masterson closed the door behind them and turned to face her. How could she have gotten herself into this conversation? she wondered.

"I have a question about a personal matter," she managed to say, thankfully without stammering.

Bat was likely wondering what trail she'd led him down, but he was gentleman enough to spread his hands agreeably. "What can I tell you?"

Committed now, Prudence could only push ahead. "It concerns you and your wife."

"Emma." Masterson smiled. "I'm sure she'd like you."

"I'd enjoy meeting her. Does she ever object when you are away for long periods or time, or when you take jobs that might put your life in danger?" There—she had asked it.

Masterson grinned faintly, but without mockery. Prudence was certain he could read what was behind her question. But he answered without comment or quip.

"She knew well enough what she was getting when she accepted my proposal: a sporting man, a drifter, a troubleshooter, and sometime lawman with a reputation that keeps me looking over my shoulder. But she knew I loved her, and I guess she loved me enough to accept my way of life." Bat's tone grew thoughtful. "And I must say, she's done a pretty fair job of taming me down. Without her, I reckon I would've been bushwhacked from some dark alley, or shot over a hand of cards years ago." His eyes came back to her, and he grinned gently. "Does that answer your question?"

Prudence realized her breath had caught in her throat. "Yes," she whispered almost to herself, "I think it does."

Chapter Ten

"It ain't like I thought it would be," Thomas said. His battered features were bleak. "I've whipped up on men I've fought before, whipped up on them bad when I had to, when it meant saving my life, or keeping me or somebody else from getting hurt. And I had to whip that fellow this afternoon—had to or he might've killed me.

"But I had nothing against him, and I don't figure he had anything personal against me. We was fighting for money, and so all them high rollers and Eastern big shots could sit back and enjoy it." He shook his head. "I won the prize; now I just wish I could wash my hands of it. It's dirty money if you ask me—tainted."

Stark kept his face expressionless. Thomas was

learning something Stark himself had learned long ago. Fisticuffs for sport and for prize money, with rules and a referee, was one thing. But when you got paid to fight for life or death, and there was no justice to your cause, you were no better than the sorriest lawbreaker.

Thomas gave a shake of his heavy shoulders. "Come on," he muttered. "They're ready for you in the ring." He led the way into the huge circus-style tent that had been erected on the prairie. The dry night wind plucked at the flaps as they entered.

Noise and dust and smoke washed over them in a foul wave. The hoarse sounds of revelry enveloped them. The crowd had grown since Thomas had fought his bout that afternoon. A steady influx of carriages, horsemen, and a special coach transporting passengers from private trains arriving at the Yanger homestead, had swelled the ranks of the spectators. Stark saw everything from Eastern high rollers to two-bit hardcases who had come to see two men fight like wild beasts for their pleasure. No, Stark corrected himself, not even wild beasts could match the ferocity of mankind.

Ignoring the din, he glanced about the rows of packed benches encircling the raised ring. As he had this afternoon, he looked for, but failed to spot, the jaunty figure of Bat Masterson.

Had Masterson gotten word of the fight? he questioned, not for the first time. While Stark could likely have managed to evade the training camp guards without being detected, there was no way he could've stayed gone long enough to get a message to Bat without his absence being noticed. He'd been forced to rely on the veteran gambler's ability to learn of the match through the sources he had cultivated among Guthrie's sporting crowd. If Masterson hadn't made it here, he calculated grimly, there'd have to be some changes in his own plans.

"Kill him, Peacemaker!" a nicely dressed woman screamed at him from the front ranks of the crowd. Her heavyset male companion laughed drunkenly at her depraved desires. Sweat streamed from under his derby hat.

"Heathens," Thomas said bitterly.

Stark had seen Thomas win his brutal bout against a skilled opponent. Although Thomas had spared his foe once he'd managed to batter him senseless, Stark had no doubt but that, had the tables been turned, Thomas would not have left the ring alive. Fighting fist and boot was everything it was promoted to be. Thomas was pretty clearly having second thoughts about letting himself get roped into it.

So was Stark. He only hoped Masterson was lurking hereabouts and hadn't run into trouble somewhere along the trail.

He put any further concerns about Masterson

aside. He'd have enough worries once he climbed in that ring up ahead.

Blake Gar, the reigning champion of this misbegotten arena, had yet to make his entrance. Stark still knew little enough about him and his tactics, although he had his suspicions. He had met his opponent at a brief palaver with the Yanger boys and the two bullwhip experts who would serve as referees.

As tall as Stark, Gar gave the impression of wiry power. His thin, brooding face showed few of the scars that might've been expected on a champion prizefighter. But then most of his fights were said to end fast, mighty fast, with his opponent unable to ever fight again.

Sload appeared as Stark and Thomas reached the ring. His bulging eyes glittered. "There's half a million in house bets alone riding on this," he gloated. "And probably that much in side wagers as well!"

Despite all he'd seen and heard, Stark was a little stunned by the figures. High rollers, for sure, he thought. "What are the odds?" he asked aloud.

"Two to one." Sload paused before adding, "Against you. Folks know of you more as a gunman than a prizefighter."

"Where's your money?"

"You'll find out if you win."

"I haven't seen the Yanger boys."

"They're around." Sload turned to Thomas. "Nice win this afternoon."

Thomas grunted.

Sload's thick lips curled down in a frown. Stark vaulted up onto the ring platform. Thomas scrambled after him.

Looking out over the crowd, Stark still couldn't spot Masterson or the Yanger brothers. But he did see Blake Gar, accompanied by a half-dozen hardcases, walking with light-footed steps toward the ring. He had a wicked grin or smile or snarl or something else altogether that he bestowed on the spectators cheering his appearance.

Thomas pulled Stark's robe off his shoulders. Stark shifted his feet, trying to get used to the cheap hard-soled workboots he'd been given. The fight really was going to be with fist and boot, he reflected. For their purpose, the footwear was plenty good. With them a man could do a lot of damage to an opponent's body.

The announcer called the fighters and their attendants to the center of the ring. The crowd quieted, but still rumbled and growled under its breath. Stark came face-to-face with his foe. Gar's dark eyes— black as a bat's wings—kept flicking over him as if seeking out vulnerable points.

"A fight to the finish, ladies and gentlemen," the announcer bellowed. "Nothing barred. The winner is the last man left standing, or the last man left alive!"

Stark stopped listening to the man's blather. He felt a lightness coming over his muscles, a nettling of his nerves and sinews. A grim eagerness flared in him.

"Fist and boot! Fist and boot!" the crowd took up a surging ranting chant that rang with the pagan barbarism of ages past. The words were quickly lost, merging into a savage paean for blood and violence. Even Stark, for all the years he'd spent plying his mercenary trade, felt a cold chill touch every inch of his body.

The announcer waved the fighters back to their corners. Stark spared a glance for each of the whip-toting referees. They were stationed just outside the ropes at the other two corners of the ring. If a man didn't fight, he would taste the whip, and the crowd would probably love it.

The bell rang. The crowd went dead silent for a pair of heartbeats. Stark felt Thomas's powerful hand grip his shoulder in encouragement, then he was moving forward to meet his foe.

Gar came with his fists up like a scientific boxer of the Jim Corbett mold. Stark watched those fists, but he watched the rest of the man as well, and when the attack came, it wasn't with the fists at all.

Gar's lead foot lashed out in a vicious crippling sweep at Stark's kneecap. Hard on its heels the forked fingers of the champion's right hand snaked between Stark's guard and stabbed at his eyes. The feral ferocity of the attack was startling even to Stark. He twisted his leg to take the numbing impact of the kick on his calf, bobbed his head so the jabbing fingers landed above his eyes. He struck with his right fist, but Gar, sneering with bared teeth, tilted his body back out of range and pivoted to the outside.

Stark wheeled to catch him. Gar thrust up a distracting knee, then rammed the heel of his palm up, aiming at the base of Stark's nose. It was a blow meant to kill. Barely in time, Stark jerked his head aside. He felt Gar's hand rasp past his cheek. Right and left he punched, but met only empty air.

Stark had his answer now; his suspicions had been on the money. Blake was a dirty-tricks artist, using underhanded moves culled from fighting styles all over the world. No prolonged punching and kicking and grappling matches for him; he relied on the quick, nasty strike designed to maim or kill in an instant.

It was no wonder his bouts never lasted long. His brutal and overwhelming tactics would be too much for even highly skilled fighters. They had been the undoing of Gar's prior opponents, and had bid fair to being the undoing of Stark himself.

In the ring Gar was all movement—bobbing, weaving, ducking even when no punches were coming his way. Only his baleful smirk remained unchanged.

Stark decided to give him something to block or evade. With no warning, no cocking of his leg, Stark snapped out his lead foot. It was a good move; against even many trained fighters it would've been effective. But somehow against Gar, Stark didn't expect it to land. It didn't. Gar shifted easily clear of its reach. Stark pivoted and kicked with his other foot, spun and drove his opposite foot rearward. He went after Gar in a whirling flurry of flashing, flying kicks, using savate, the French art of foot fighting at which he was a master.

And Gar, circling about the ring, twisting, dodging, and weaving with serpentine ease, stayed just outside his range.

Hang him! Stark thought. He was as elusive as a dust devil. And the instant Stark let up, the second he halted his attack, Gar would be on him with another of his devilish tricks.

Gauging the moment, Stark turned his last roundhouse kick into a complete spin, springing backward a good three feet to land balanced and on guard, fists up.

Counting on a heartbeat's vulnerability, Gar checked his rush. The hesitation seemed only a feint, for he lunged in. His left hand caught Stark's wrist and twisted his arm aside with surprising strength. In close, Gar struck twice, Japanese style—

a slashing crossover edge of the hand blow at the side of the neck, then the stiffened fingers of the same hand driving Stark's throat. Stark used his left arm to foul both blows.

But Gar wasn't done yet. Against a half-dozen more efforts to blind, cripple, or kill him with heel, knee, fist, and skull, Stark defended. Some came close. Stark could sense the hot, harsh expectancy of the crowd like the tingling charge before a bolt of summer lighting. Gar's arsenal of infighting tricks seemed endless, but at last Stark saw a glittering of determination in the onyx eyes, and knew he'd outlasted any other opponent Gar had faced.

The champion's next strike came like a double bolt of that summer lightning. Gar's open hands streaked for Stark's neck. Pain jolted through Stark's system. Dimly he understood that the next move would have Gar pivoting about so they were back-to-back, then snapping Stark's neck across his shoulder.

Desperate, Stark clamped his left hand over his right fist and rammed his locked arms upward. Gar's clawing grip was torn from his throat. Trained reflex brought Stark's doubled fists crashing back down. They hammered the top of Gar's skillfully ducked head rather than the bridge of his nose as Stark had hoped. But the impact was yet enough to buckle the champion's knees, and to give Stark time for a dirty trick of his own.

Simultaneously his right hand drove at Gar's face, his left fist thrust below the V of Gar's ribs, and his knee surged up at Gar's lower body. The whole lunging force of his body was behind the moves.

It was called the three-pronger, taught to Stark long ago by an old sailor on the docks of New York. Properly done, there was no way for anyone, even Blake Gar, to guard against all three moves at once.

But Gar did his best. The stiffened fingers he dodged with a sideward twitch of his head. The other two thrusts drove home and sent Gar, doubled over, reeling back across the ring.

The blood roar of the crowd broke over Stark. *Now!* he thought, before Gar had a chance to recover and trot out some other devil-spawned trick. He took a single long stride and launched himself into the air, twisting to pack every bit of power he could behind the booted foot. Gar fell sprawling and Stark landed crouched beside his supine form.

The tumult of the crowd seemed to vibrate the walls of the tent. Stark straightened and stepped clear of Gar's spread-eagled shape. He noted the slow rise and fall of the fighter's chest and felt a rush of relief that he hadn't killed this man to satisfy the bloodthirsty onlookers.

The noise of the crowd began to take on a demanding rhythmic tone. It was a moment before Stark understood just what they were demanding, and then he felt the blood turn to ice in his veins. The spectators were urging him to finish the job. They wanted to see a killing.

Stark gazed about him at the mass of ugly, eager faces. He kept his face as rigid as stone so none of the feelings of contempt and revulsion rolling through him could be detected. He needed the favor of the crowd for leverage in the next stage of the scheme he and Masterson had hatched. But he wasn't going to commit murder to get it.

Still, he had to do something. The crowd might easily turn on him. He had beaten their favorite, and a lot of them had lost money on his victory. The referees were fingering their whips. A lynching of the victor wasn't entirely out of the question.

Swiftly he bent and locked his fingers on Gar's form. Then with a single heaving effort he straightened and lifted the limp shape of the fighter up over his head. Holding him like that, joints and arms burning with the strain, he strutted once around the ring. Then he cast Gar contemptuously back to the floor.

The crowd loved the grotesque display. It bellowed barbaric approval. Stark turned and strode to his corner. Thomas scrambled through the ropes to meet him. Behind him a nattily-suited figure clambered onto the platform.

Stark couldn't hear over the crowd, but he saw Bat Masterson's mouth form the sardonic words, "Nice job."

Chapter Eleven

"You figure our new pard you hooked us up with can be trusted?" Bat asked, sitting in the saddle with familiar ease.

Their horses were moving at a lazy canter across the sea of buffalo grass under the midmorning sun. "If he couldn't, we'd never have left that fight tent alive," Stark said. "Thomas has had his bellyful of fist and boot, and it ain't setting well with him. He won't blindside us when push comes to shove."

Masterson grunted noncommittally. He'd stood by skeptically the night before when, during the hubbub after the fight, Stark had drawn Thomas aside and recruited him to the cause.

Stark had acted almost on impulse, but still this morning it seemed to him a good idea to have Thomas siding them. The prizefighter had listened with widening eyes as Stark related his reasons for being involved in the fight business, and the role Masterson played in the scheme.

"We might need you to cover our backs or act as a go-between with the U.S. Marshal in Guthrie," Stark had finished. "You game?"

Thomas hadn't hesitated long. "I made up my mind during your fight that I needed to get out of this sorry business. It's the devil's doings. I'm your man. I'll ride with you fellows all the way."

"How much farther to the Yanger homeplace?" Masterson broke in on Stark's reflections.

"Couple of miles."

"How we going to brace them?"

"Straight up. Clint will be curious enough that he'll want to hear what we have to say. That'll get us inside. No telling which way Burt will jump. He's a hothead."

"Supposed to be mighty quick with a gun."

"An amateur," Stark said derisively. "He does it for fun."

Masterson grimaced. "Nothing worse."

They halted when they came in full sight of the homeplace. Stark waited while Masterson gave it a once-over. There were fewer gunmen loitering about than on Stark's prior visit. Most of the pack had been at the fight last night and were likely sleeping it off in the bunkhouse. Some of the high rollers probably occupied rooms in the house itself.

Finished with his appraisal, Bat glanced over at Stark. "How's your gun hand?"

"I didn't hit him more than two or three times," Stark reminded dryly. "It's fine."

Masterson nodded. "Let's deal," he said curtly, and jigged his horse forward.

As they neared the house Stark saw Chad, the tall gunhawk ramrod, appear with another hombre who was quickly dispatched to the house. Chad himself sauntered forward and mounted the porch. He was waiting when they drew rein.

"I'll be blamed if you didn't do it," he drawled at Stark with an edge of admiration. "You're a regular bearcat with or without all them guns."

Stark accepted the compliment with a brief nod.

Chad's gaze shuttled to Bat and held there a moment. "You'd be Masterson."

"The same," Bat admitted.

"Reckon the two of you are here to see the boss men."

"That's a fact," Star confirmed.

"Yeah, they were kind of expecting you, Peacemaker." He looked meaningfully at Masterson. "Alone."

Stark hitched his shoulders. "They got us both."

"I reckon." Chad flicked a glance over his shoulder as his message boy emerged from the house and gave a nod. Chad jerked his head toward the door. "Go on in. They'll see you."

They were received in the big den with the up-holstered chairs and fancy bar. The ivory-featured female bartender was absent. Clint played the role of gracious host while Burt prowled, eyeing them suspiciously. Bat accepted the offer of whiskey. He sipped it as he exchanged wary pleasantries with Clint. Stark stayed on his feet and kept an eye on Burt.

"Well, Stark, I expect you'll be wanting your cut of the take." Clint got down to business at last. "You certainly earned it. There's only one other man I've ever seen fight like you did. I can give you part of your share now in cash and a draft for the rest when it's collected, if that's satisfactory."

"It'll do for now," Stark told him.

Clint's cigar and eyebrow went up inquiringly. The affability slipped off of him like the skin off a snake. "What's that supposed to mean?"

"What it means is that he's got a new partner," Masterson interjected. "Me. And since I hold the top fighter, it also means that I hold the whiphand in the fist and boot fights."

Stark watched it slowly sink in on Clint. "Well, I'll be hanged," he said at last. "Of all the brass-bound nerve, you take the prize, Masterson. I had a gut feeling you two were in cahoots. I should've trusted it and put you out of action."

"Too late now," Masterson told him. "You and sonny boy here can have a couple of days to pack up, but then you'll need to hit the trail. I don't figure you have any legitimate legal title to these land holdings, but I'll give you, say, five thousand dollars for the whole outfit, lock, stock, and barrel."

The proposal was so outrageous that it actually held Clint transfixed for a span of heartbeats. Masterson was pushing for a showdown, and he wasn't wasting any time doing it.

"Who in thunder do you think you're talking to, you tinhorn?" It was actually Burt who recovered first.

"I told you once not to fool around with the professionals, sonny," Stark said to draw the lightning.

He drew it all right. Burt wheeled toward him, crouched almost like a wrestler, hands hovering near his waist. His brother might've made a move to stop him, but he never got the chance.

"I'm no amateur! Try your luck, Peacemaker!"

Burt's right hand dipped and came up with his pistol; his left streaked across his body to heel back the hammer with the butt of his palm. Stark was set for him. The calloused base of his hand had given him away when Stark had first met him. He was a gun-fanner, and, expecting it, Stark sidestepped as his own hand swooped. He had to pull, cock, and trigger the .45, but its blast still merged thunderously with Burt's fanned shot. The bullet drilled the air where Stark had just stood. For a fanner, Burt was plenty good. Through wreaths of smoke, Stark saw him reel back with the shoulder of his gun arm flapping loosely.

While Burt was still collapsing, Masterson came smoothly out of his chair and stepped swiftly side-wise so he could see all of the room and yet keep Clint in the edge of his vision. He made no move to draw his gun from beneath his coat. Other than to snarl with anger, the elder Yanger didn't move from his seat. He had a tense air of waiting.

He didn't have to wait long. The ramrod, Chad, must not have gone far. He burst into the room at the head of a pack of a dozen hardcases.

They drew up sharply at the scene before them. Gun leveled, Stark stood awaiting them with Curt's weakly sobbing form beyond. Masterson had yet to pull his pistol, but the lethal menace radiating from his trim dark figure was somehow as chilling as the ominous barrel of Stark's smoking .45.

"What in blue blazes?" the ramrod blurted. There were no guns showing among his crew.

Yet.

"Rest easy, gentlemen," Masterson advised. "We're just having a little confab with the boss men."

For a long handful of seconds it could've gone either way. A last wisp of smoke still trailed up from the barrel of Stark's levelled Colt, and the harsh smell of burned powder hung strong in the room. Stark longed for his lever-action shotgun. With it, he could've cleared the room if lead started to fly. But toting it into a business meeting would've tipped their hand. His .38 Marlin hideout was in reserve. It was his two pistols and Masterson's shoulder-hung revolver against a dozen hired guns.

But added to their weapons were the reputations both he and Masterson had earned over the years. It was as much those reps—the specters of dead men both real and fancied—as the guns that held Chad and his crew at bay.

"Go on, blast you!" Clint Yanger found his voice at last. "Cut them down! There's only two of them!"

"That's right." Somehow Masterson's sibilant whisper carried. "Only two."

Slowly Chad began to rotate his head back and forth on his neck. His eyes were on Stark's Colt, but when he spoke, it was to his boss. "I reckon not," he said bitterly. "I hired on to risk my life if need be, but I sure as the devil didn't hire on to throw it away."

Stark was watching all of them. Chad's decision would carry the majority, but there was generally one in the crowd who had to be contrary, maybe looking for a reputation of his own. Stark's eye caught the darting movement of a hand among the rear ranks of the group. He swiveled his wrist, and cocked and fired.

The gunhawk's hand never touched his weapon. He folded hard in the middle and collapsed. Other than shifting his wrist, Stark hadn't moved. "Next up," he said coolly.

There were no takers. A murmur of awed curses and exclamations ran through the cluster of hard-cases. When he was sure it was finished, Stark jerked his head toward Burt's crumpled form. "Get him out of here and tend to him. The other one, too, if he's not beyond tending. All of you clear out."

Grudgingly they complied. When the last of them had disappeared Stark shifted his full attention to Clint.

Outwardly the elder Yanger had regained his composure. "Thanks for just winging the kid," he said tightly, and sipped at his whiskey with a hand that trembled only a hair. "You probably did him a favor. He was fixing to get himself killed looking for gunfights."

"My pleasure," Stark said dryly.

Yanger cocked his head and regarded Masterson. He had the air of a man with an ace up his sleeve. "You're talking to the wrong fellow."

"How's that?" Masterson demanded.

"I'm just the manager for the head honchos back East." Clint gave his head a rueful shake. "I used to think I pulled some weight until I ran into them."

Stark felt his nostrils flare. He'd just gotten the first scent of his prey.

"Who are we talking about?" Masterson inquired.

Yanger considered a moment before answering. "Benjamin Standard for one. There's others, almost as powerful. They've formed a sort of combine that has invested heavily in this enterprise, among other things. I set this operation up with their backing."

"Sounds like that makes you expendable," Masterson commented.

"Does it? Think again. It's my organization that makes this work. Without me you'd be starting from scratch. And I've already got the trust of Standard and his cronies. You could try to run the fist and boot fights without me, but I promise you it wouldn't be as efficient or nearly as profitable."

Yanger's cooperation would make things a sight easier, so long as he didn't suspect their real reason for cutting in on the operation, Stark knew. He figured Masterson would reach the same conclusion, but he spoke aloud just the same. "He's talking some sense, Bat."

Masterson nodded absently. "Just what are you proposing, Yanger?"

Stark could tell Clint reckoned he had regained some control of the situation. His smile was as amiable as that of a snake oil salesman. And that was just about as far as he could be trusted.

"Let's say we have a truce, albeit an armed one," Yanger gave answer to Masterson's question. "Maybe it can develop into a partnership. I've seen your man fight twice, and I want a piece of him. Folks are going to be demanding to see more of what he can do. Of course, Stark, there'd be even bigger opportunities if you'd see fit to finish what you start in the ring, instead of leaving your opponents alive, if not exactly kicking."

"I'll work on it," Stark growled.

"And I'll get Standard and the rest of them out here pronto for a confab. They'll have to approve of you as a business associate, Masterson, and of you, Stark, as a fighter." Yanger's grin had an evil glint to it.

Stark knew what Yanger hadn't bothered to mention. Approval of him depended on how well he did against whatever top-notch fighter Standard and the others brought with them. He would be a spoiler— an hombre who made his brutal living whipping upstarts like Stark. A beating in the ring would substanially weaken the bargaining position he and Masterson had, and give the Eastern bosses the reins to the whole operation once more.

Stark felt a wicked eagerness to face this unknown champion. He tamped the ugly sensation down. The illicit fight game, for all its savagery and brutality, had a seductive allure to it. He'd do well to guard against its pull. Besides, if their plan worked out, Nix and his men would corral the whole bunch of Yanger and his bosses before a private bout between him if their spoiler ever took place.

Still, if it happened, he doubted he would ever face a tougher opponent. . . .

"Then it's agreed," Yanger was summarizing. "I'll call my boys off so you won't have to watch your backs."

Masterson snorted contemptuously.

"Of course, both of you will need to stick around—either here at the homeplace, or out at one of the camps. Understood?"

Masterson gave a nod of affirmation. "Just don't drag your feet," he warned.

Once they were outside Bat cut a shrewd glance at Stark. "Did you get lucky or are you good enough to wing Burt on purpose?"

"A little of both," Stark told him. "I didn't want him dead because then Clint might be more interested in lifting our scalps than in making a deal with us."

Masterson gave a wry grin. "Deal or no, my scalp doesn't feel safe just yet."

Chapter Twelve

"Any word yet?" Prudence asked more eagerly than she'd intended.

If Evett Nix noticed, he didn't let on. He was looking a bit trail-worn himself, Prudence reflected. The strain was slowly sawing at their nerves. What would it be like, she asked herself again, to be married to a man—Jim—whose trade often kept him away on missions from which he might not return?

"Nothing yet," Nix told her as he rose and came from behind his desk to greet her. He didn't bother with any reassuring platitudes, for which Prudence was grateful. "Join me?" He gestured at the seating arrangement of upholstered chairs that graced his office.

"Thank you."

She was too edgy to really relax, but she sipped at the tart cider he offered.

"I saw your latest column," he commented. "Another nice piece."

She had written it with the unstated hope that it might generate the same kind of response as her second one had. But the well-mannered Mr. Tallant and his cold-eyed bodyguard had yet to make another appearance.

Since Bat's departure upon learning of the scheduled fight between Jim and someone named Gar, she had trod an ever-narrowing mountain path of worry, frustration, and anger. Sometimes she herself was the focus of that anger.

"If nothing breaks in the next couple of days I'll send Heck Thomas or Bill Tilghman out to see the Yanger boys." Nix's voice pulled her back from the edge of that path.

"Is that wise?" Prudence asked. "If either of them question the Yanger brothers, they're bound to become suspicious. It could make things even more dangerous for Jim and Bat." *That was just like a lawyer,* she berated herself mentally. She had to play devil's advocate even when she'd be more than pleased to see Tilghman or Thomas, or both of them, go and check on Jim.

"I'd tell whoever I sent to ride easy," Nix said. "Just take a look-see and not stir things up."

Prudence pressed her white teeth into her lower

lip. "And none of your men have heard anything about another fight?" she asked without much hope.

Nix shook his head doggedly from side to side. "Nary a hint of it on the gambling circuit. Whatever's going on, it's apparently a private party."

Prudence gave a resigned sigh. "Very well." She made to rise. "Thank you, Evett. I'm sure you'll keep me informed."

Nix rose hurriedly. "It's getting late. Would you care to join Ellen and me for dinner?"

She knew he was doing his best to keep her mind off the uncertainties of Jim's well-being, and, truthfully, his invitation was tempting.

Friends since childhood, Evett and his bride had finally tied the knot and journeyed down from Kansas to take part in the famed Land Run of '89 which had opened Oklahoma Territory for settlement. They were a charming and gracious couple, and their company would be a pleasant diversion.

But, on second thought, the idea of spending the evening with them by herself, while her concerns over Jim's fate were weighing so heavily upon her, seemed not so appealing after all. Just why that was so, she wasn't certain. Could it be the faint sense of heartache and loneliness she often felt of late when in the presence of a happy and satisfied couple such as Evett and Ellen Nix?

"Not tonight, Evett; thank you." She smiled

sweetly to let him know she did appreciate the offer. "I'd best be getting back to my office."

That might uncharitably be characterized as a lie, she chided herself. There was nothing urgent awaiting her. But there were projects that could keep her busy. They might even take her mind off James Stark for longer than a pair of seconds.

She beat a hasty retreat from the lawman's presence. Back in her own office she busied herself with the odds and ends of catch-up work that always lurked in a busy lawyer's practice: reviewing draft documents, checking statute cites in briefs and opinions, returning routine correspondence.

Martha had left when the office had formally closed for the day, so she had only herself and her work for company. *How many other lonely evenings and weekends had that been the case?* she wondered, then reined her mind sharply back to the dry legal prose in front of her.

The clock on her desk ticked loudly. The flames in the lamps burned steadily. In the slow fading of the light they cast, she was remotely aware of the growing gloom beyond the windows as it crept inward.

For a moment she thought her ears had played a trick on her, and that she'd only imagined the sound of the door in the outer office being eased open. Then the tinkling peal of the bell connected to it made her start so abruptly that her pen scratched a trail of ink across the document she'd been reviewing.

By the time she stood up, automatically pulling her right hand drawer open as she rose, an unwelcome figure loomed in the doorway of her office.

"Prudence! I'm glad I caught you here."

"What do you want, Mr. Tallant? And we're not on a first-name basis." She put as much ice as she could into her tones.

Benjamin Standard's agent and spokesman smiled his charming, boyish smile. "Oh, we're far past formalities. Call me Art. And to answer your question, business brought me back to Guthrie, and I wanted the chance to renew our acquaintance." Unbidden, he strode confidently into the room.

"I have office hours, Mr. Tallant," she advised, keeping her teeth pressed tightly together as she spoke.

Her hostility seemed to bounce right off of him. "I was hoping for something of a less businesslike nature," he declared, and posed handsomely in his tailored suit.

She was playing with a live rattlesnake, she knew. But the desire to try to obtain more information about his influential employer was strong enough to make her resist the urge to demand that he leave. The office building was probably all but deserted by now, so she was on her own. But she could handle the likes of him.

She hoped.

"I'm afraid any sort of social relationship is out of the question right now." She let her voice thaw a few degrees. "But I have had time to think over the proposal you made at our last meeting."

He arched his eyebrows with evident interest. "Is that a fact? Well, by all means let's discuss business and set personal matters aside for the nonce." He dropped into one of the client chairs before her desk.

Prudence stayed on her feet. She felt safer with the ability to move quickly. And besides, standing while others were seated was always a good ploy for keeping the upper hand in any sort of meeting.

He smiled as though he recognized her tactic and wasn't particularly discomfitted by it.

"Where's Mr. Lecker?" she asked archly.

Tallant uttered a single-syllable chuckle. "Oh, I didn't want him along tonight. He's poor company even when he's not working."

"How did you know I was here?"

"That was easy enough. I checked at your hotel and they informed me that you hadn't been in yet. The clerk even commented that you often work late. So I took a chance on finding you here and got lucky." A wicked gleam flashed in his eyes. "Now, tell me what conclusions you've reached about our offer."

"I may be interested in accepting it."

"What happened to your conflict of interest?"

"It's been resolved." Watching him, Prudence couldn't tell if he believed her or not. The glitter in his eyes made it plain enough what his main motive was, but he seemed willing enough to mix business with pleasure if the opportunity presented itself.

"That's very interesting," he commented. "So you now see your way clear to accepting the retainer?"

"Perhaps. But first I would need to know more about your principal's business interests and goals in this area."

"That's easy enough: to acquire assets and power in the territories."

"Does he already have holdings here or in the Indian lands?"

"I'm not privy to the full scope of his enterprises," he evaded her neatly. "Frankly, tonight I'm more concerned with my own interests and desires, and how they might merge with your own."

Tread carefully, girl, she told herself. "I have no interest in permanent mergers," she told him aloud.

"Indeed? Well, there's always the option of short-term associations. They can be most satisfying for both parties." He rose easily from his chair.

"I think our business together is over," Prudence said flatly.

For a couple of heartbeats he stood very still, as if frozen in mid-motion. In those two beats of time his face turned as hard and cold as a stone in a blizzard.

"And I think you've just been playing games with me, honey. Mr. Standard didn't like your latest column. Since we were already in this sorry part of creation, he sent me to tell you of his dislike. He said I was to make very sure you understand how much he objects to your columns. I decided that I could have myself a little fun while I delivered his message."

Leering, he stepped around the corner of her desk toward her.

Prudence's hand darted down into the open desk drawer and came up with the .32 revolver she kept there. A gift from James Stark, it was double-action, so she didn't have to ear back the hammer in order to fire. She did it anyway for the ominous click it made in the office. Being around Jim had taught her all kinds of things she once wouldn't have deigned to learn. But just now that click sounded mighty reassuring to her.

Tallant drew up short. He didn't look scared, only cautious, she realized with a touch of fear of her own.

"Stay where you are," she ordered coolly.

He took another small step and halted, but he was now within arm's reach of her. She fought the impulse to step back. She sensed it might only precipitate a lunge toward her.

She didn't want to shoot him; she had expected the gun to frighten him. But he was far from frightened. In fact, if the flare of his patrician nostrils was any indication, he was enjoying this brush with danger. In that moment she understood that he saw her as some sort of prize, and she understood too that she might have to shoot him after all. Her heart shrank from the prospect, but her hand remained firm on the gun.

"Now, you don't really think I can't defend myself against a little girl with a toy gun, do you?" he jeered.

"Don't know about that," a lazy masculine voice drawled from the doorway. "But you might better be concerned about defending yourself against me."

Tallant swung sharply about and Prudence stole a darting glance at the speaker. She didn't recognize the dusky, powerfully built man framed in the doorway, but she was dearly glad to see him just the same.

He advanced into the office with a rolling stride. His faded denims and workshirt didn't conceal the breadth of his shoulders or the powerful flex of muscles beneath the heavy fabric. He wasn't carrying a gun.

"What are you doing here, boy?" Tallant snarled.

"Just wanted to talk to the lady. Reckon you best leave now. Looks to me like she don't want to talk with you, or do much of anything else with you, for that matter."

Tallant stepped clear of the desk. "You've made a mistake, boy," he advised. "But I'm going to enjoy correcting you." He stripped off his coat and raised his fists in a pugilist's stance. He had some muscles of his own.

A slow grin spread across the newcomer's dark features. "Well, well," he mused with cold mirth. "What do we have here? You been sparring in the athletic clubs with the other *gentlemen,* have you?"

"The Excelsior in New York," affirmed Tallant with no small amount of pride. "And I've trained and sparred with some of the best boxers in the world."

"Is that a fact? Well, why don't you just show this poor old boy how it's done?"

The stranger lifted his own fists—big scarred ones—in a workmanlike contrast to Tallant's posed stance. Recognition flickered in Prudence's mind. She had seen the stranger in such a posture before—at the illicit prizefight to which Jim had escorted her on behalf of her client. This man had been one of the contenders!

She had no time to analyze the knowledge. Spurred on by the fellow's taunts in front of a woman, Tallant poked his left fist straight out and followed it with an arcing right hand. Prudence felt a wisp of thoroughly wicked pleasure at what she suspected was about to take place.

The prizefighter made a little shuffling movement with his feet, hunched his bull shoulders, and pulled his head down. Tallant's lift slipped past his ear, and his right curled past his skull. The stranger put shoulder and body behind a slashing counter right hand that ripped in under Tallant's heart. Tallant's entire torso bent sideways, contorting him almost into a U shape. And the newcomer's right hand powered upward in a blurred course that met Tallant's manly jaw with an impact that made Prudence wince.

And just like that it was over. Four punches had been thrown; two had landed. Amateur against professional. Prudence felt a twinge of conscience over her wicked longing of a moment before as Tallant dropped to the floor of her office like her desk had fallen on top of him. He didn't move, and it was with relief that she saw the slow rise and fall of his chest.

"That's the difference between sparring and fighting, boy," his conqueror said.

Prudence lifted her gaze to him. "Thank you," she said sincerely. "I don't know what would've happened if you hadn't arrived."

A broad grin split his face. "Reckon I just saved this fellow's life. Not likely he'll be beholding to me, though, I'm guessing. My name's Thomas Sampson, ma'am."

Prudence looked at the revolver in her small fist, then put it resolutely back into the drawer. "I'm Prudence McKay."

"I was pretty sure of that before I busted in. The Peacemaker said there'd be no mistaking you."

"You have some word from Jim?" she blurted. "Is he all right?"

"He's just fine, and so's Mr. Masterson. They sent me to give you and Marshal Nix word that it's getting awful close to the final round."

Involuntarily Prudence glanced at Tallant's crumpled form. That explained why his boss was in the Territories. Jim and Bat Masterson had succeeded in drawing the Eastern sponsors out of their lairs. They were ruthless and powerful men, with Lecker and no doubt other killers of his ilk at their beck and call.

She thought of Thomas's appropriate metaphor. The last round was drawing near. And that meant, staying with the metaphor, that she and Evett Nix needed to move fast to be sure Jim Stark wasn't going to go down for his final count.

Chapter Thirteen

"Reckon I'll take another look around," Stark advised.

Masterson glanced up from the game of solitaire in which he was methodically beating himself. "Say hello to the Yanger crew," he requested dryly.

"My pleasure."

But the hired guns were still keeping their distance from the training camp cabin where he and Masterson had holed up, he saw as he stepped out into the coolness of the prairie night. Chad and a handful of other gunhawks were roosting in the bunkhouse on the other side of the camp.

Their presence was pretty much a token gesture. If he and Masterson really wanted to head out, either openly or under cover of night, then Chad and his pards weren't going to be able to stop them. Nor, Stark mused, were any of them really hankering to give it a try. Besides, with the stakes riding on the meeting scheduled for tomorrow, he and Bat would be fools for cutting out now, no matter what their motives in setting up the palaver.

The wait had stretched Stark's nerves as taut as new strung barbed wire. He envied Masterson his seeming coolness. But in the grim determination with which he duelled himself with the pasteboards, even the older man's tension was starting to show.

There'd been no word from Thomas since he'd departed on the mission Stark had given him. Nothing surprising in that, Stark knew. Once he'd gotten word to Prudence and Evett, there'd be no way Thomas could make it back here any faster than Nix and his posse.

If he'd gotten word to them . . .

Restlessly Stark turned toward the corral. He'd check on Red. The roar of a shot and the spike of flame in his direction rent the darkness. Taut nerves and a gunman's reflexes dropped Stark flat. His arm hooked to pull the Colt even as he moved. Recoil jarred his wrist once before his chest hit the ground, then twice more in the split-second following.

He heard a cry and saw a flurry of movement at the corner of the shed where the bushwhacker's gun had blazed. He rolled over twice, lining his gun with

outstretched arm as he came out of it once more flat
on his belly.

His ears were ringing but he still could hear the
muffled sounds from the dark shape lying on the
ground. Whoever it was had been waiting there in
ambush. God's grace that he'd turned toward the
corral when he had, Stark thought reverently.

Behind him the cabin door opened. "Jim?" came
Masterson's terse voice. He hadn't emerged from
the structure. Gun drawn, he was crouched, peering
around the doorjamb.

"One over by the shed," Stark advised in a harsh
whisper. "He's down. I think he's the only one."

"Cover me." Masterson slipped out of the cabin
like a wraith, darted off to one side and dropped to
one knee.

No shots greeted him. The gunhawks were starting to emerge from the bunkhouse. Shouted inquir-
ies sounded. Rising, Stark legged it swiftly to his
fallen victim. He wanted some answers before the
gunsels crowded in.

"Keep them back!" he tossed over his shoulder
to Masterson.

"Keno," came Masterson's reply.

A strangled voice issued from the shape on the
ground. "Hang you, Stark! You ruined me first, and
now you've killed me!"

Stark stood over him. "You played a bad hand,
Sload," he said bitterly. He could tell the promoter

was right; he was dying. One or more of Stark's snap shots had gone home.

"The Yangers threw me out when you made your move to take over," Sload gasped. "I never done you no wrong! I've been waiting for my chance to even it up, hang you!"

"You should've cut your losses," Stark said heavily.

He'd noted that Sload seemed to have disappeared, but had given little thought to it over the past days. Now, to his grief, he'd crawled out of his hole. The man was a tinhorn and a bushwhacker, but he was right after a fashion. Stark had used him for his own ends, and then betrayed him when it suited his purposes. Maybe Sload deserved what he'd gotten for shooting from ambush, but his death left a bad taste in Stark's mouth just the same.

"Make your peace with God, Sload," he advised. There was nothing more he could do.

"Hang you, Stark." Sload was unrepentant to the end.

Shaking his head, Stark turned away from the lifeless shape. His eye fell on something and he bent to retrieve a hideout gun where it had fallen from its owner's grip. A lousy choice for a bushwhacking, Stark mused.

There was little to-do made over the killing. The hired guns shrugged Sload's death off callously. They lived and died by the gun. Sload had pulled on the wrong hombre and, even shooting from cover, hadn't been able to take him. That pretty well settled matters in their books.

"You got any regrets?" Masterson asked shrewdly when Chad and the rest had drifted away. A couple of them had toted Sload's body off to be laid in an unmarked grave.

"I'm doing better than Sload, I reckon," Stark said.

Masterson snorted. "Bet on it. Come on, we best turn in. Tomorrow morning is when we're set to meet our new Eastern partners."

The steam locomotive with its single private Pullman car and trailing caboose had arrived at the Yanger homeplace sometime during the night, Stark saw as he and Masterson rode up to the house, with the slanting rays of the morning sun at their backs.

The powers behind the fist and boot fights had wasted little time in traveling cross-country to see to their investment.

Stark scanned the surrounding countryside. The hired guns from the training camp were tagging along behind them some ways back. There was no sign of a posse of lawmen led by Evett Nix.

"Likely too soon to be expecting them," Masterson murmured as though he'd read his thoughts. He grinned tightly. "Just the same, I've been waiting to play this hand for some time."

"We're playing it without our hole card," Stark reminded him.

"I'll play it whichever it falls." Masterson urged his horse forward.

They were shown into the big sitting room with its fancy bar and mounted animal heads. No one else was present. Masterson shrugged and sauntered to the bar. He poured himself a shot and lifted the bottle inquiringly. Stark refused with a shake of his head. Masterson downed his shot, hesitated, then set the glass aside and pushed the bottle resolutely away.

Two men eased into sight from the rear of the house. Voices sounded behind them. Stark eyed the pair, and even though they were city-bred he recognized their breed. They wore dude suits and vests like businessmen, but their business was the pull of a trigger and the roar of a gun. Both were no doubt veterans of vicious gun duels and squalid shootouts in the pubs and back alleys of the big cities of the East.

The pair were an advance guard for the party that tailed them. It was a mixed bag. Clint and Burt, the latter with his arm in a sling, were playing host to a handful of Easterners. Accompanying them was a trio of women, one of them the ivory-featured bartender. She was a little the worse for wear, and looked very sad.

Three of the four Easterners had the look of aging

business czars, burdened by wealth and greed and corruption. The fourth hombre stood out from them like a hawk among crows. Involuntarily Stark pulled in air through flared nostrils. He felt his muscles tighten instinctively.

Like recognized like. From across the room the unblinking eyes of predators met and held. To Stark all of his senses seemed suddenly heightened, honed to a keen edge. There was a link between him and this stranger as real as the pulses traveling through a telegraph line.

Here was the Eastern spoiler, the champion bred in the mean streets and ruthless underworld of civilization. Even the Eastern guns seemed to shy away from him.

Stark had only half an ear for Clint Yanger's glad-handed introductions. Burt wore his pistol rigged for some kind of greenhorn crossdraw. Stark ignored his sullen glare.

Vaguely he recognized the names of the business magnates. Benjamin Standard, a cold little sidewinder of a man, was the clear ringleader. Jackson Baines was a name to conjure with in banking and railroads. The private spur serving the Yanger homestead became a little easier to understand. Baines was silver-haired. His handsome features were corrupted by dissipation of mind and body. Edison Wright was a speculator and broker of big business deals. His nod of approval was said to be able to make or break major corporate powers. From his puffy face and the suet straining the seams of his suit, he did a lot of his wheeling and dealing at fine restaurants and country club bars.

The two gunmen were Lecker and Dorn. Stark felt their appraising eyes as he and the spoiler came face to face. Remotely he heard the name Jason Boullard.

Neither of them offered to shake hands. It had been a good long spell since Stark had felt physically intimidated by another man, and he wasn't sure he felt that now. But it came mighty close.

The man called Boullard was big, bigger than Stark—taller and broader, with the kind of build that didn't show his size until he stood next to a chair or a table and it became clear. He was young enough not to have started losing his strength or reflexes, but old enough to have learned by hard experience how to use them both.

Just like Stark.

In his raggedly handsome face, Stark saw the scars of his education in unarmed fighting. None of the scars were recent.

"I understand you're the boss in the ring out here in the wilderness." Boullard's voice was edged with some sort of European accent, but his English was as precise as a clean right hook.

"Just a temporary position," Stark said. "It always is, no matter who holds it, here or elsewhere."

The corner of Boullard's mouth lifted. "You're a wise man for a common prizefighter."

He turned arrogantly away. He did it lightly, smoothly, ready to counter if he sensed a sucker punch coming his way.

Peremptorily Clint dismissed the women. They seemed eager to clear out. Standard and his cronies must party rough.

The little business tycoon straightened his rumpled suit. "Mr. Boullard is our negotiator," he said to Stark.

"I know what he is," Stark said coldly. "He's a high-dollar professional thug, a strongarm man, a skull breaker. The only sort of negotiating he'll do is in the ring with me. You brought him out here to pin my ears back. If he whips me, then our leverage in bargaining is cut in half, and I've been put in my place. I won't get too cocky, knowing you hold the leash on someone who can take me down anytime he likes."

"Very astute, Mr. Stark," Standard praised. "But I thought Mr. Masterson handled the business end of matters."

"He does. I'm just the skull breaker."

Standard pursed his thin lips contemptuously and addressed Masterson. "I've read some of your newspaper columns on sporting events. They're surprisingly well done for one of your background. You wouldn't be here just for the purpose of trying to get information for some kind of exposé, would you?" Something in the little man's tone hinted that, in his own way, he could be very dangerous.

"I'm not interested in what I could make on a story, when there's more profit to be made being a part of it," Masterson parried the probe easily. "And speaking of profit, let's get down to business here."

Stark left him to haggle with Standard and his partners. He eyed Boullard. "Kind of out of your territory, aren't you?"

"Not so much," the fighter answered almost lazily. "You might be surprised some of the places where I've fought. Then again maybe you wouldn't. I hear you use your feet. Savate?"

Stark shrugged. "A little."

Boullard grinned mirthlessly. "I'll bet. Where did you learn it?"

"An old Frenchman up in Montana taught me when I was a kid."

Boullard smirked. "A master of the art no doubt."

"Not as good as Charlemont." Stark's tone was dry.

"You studied under Joseph Charlemont?" Boullard demanded.

"For a spell when I was in Paris working for the Pinkertons."

"I studied under LeBeau."

Charlemont's renegade student—Stark recognized the name. Somehow it came as no great surprise that Boullard's skills were rooted in the French art of foot fighting and pugilism.

And he'd been trained by an expert. Stark knew the tales. Charlemont was the acknowledged master of the art. And, so the stories ran, he had taught everything he knew to Jacques LeBeau, only to have his erstwhile student turn on him and challenge him to a match. They had fought to a standstill, and LeBeau had gone into a self-imposed exile, teaching a select few students the more brutal style he himself then developed.

"Should make it interesting for the rubes," Stark commented.

"For us as well, my friend. I am looking forward to it."

And, in a dark sort of way, Stark realized, he was too.

Chapter Fourteen

Stark faced Boullard across the ring. No whip-toting referees here and no rowdy crowd, he mused; just the Yanger brothers, Standard and his bodyguards and cronies, and what had to be the bulk of the Western gunhands. This was a private bout held in an outdoor ring at one of the training camps.

A tarp had been erected to give the bigshots some shade. There was no such relief for the fighters. High noon had been chosen because both fighters would be equally handicapped by the sun glaring directly overhead. Sweat ran in runnels on their bare torsos and slid into their eyes off their foreheads.

There had been no sign of Evett or a posse, though they should've had plenty of time to get here by now, Stark calculated. Of course, he knew, if they had gone to the Yanger homestead, it might be impossible for them to find their way here to the training camp, given they knew where to look. On the plus side, if they did show up, the presence of the gunhawks as spectators meant there were few guards stationed. However, the open setting would still make it difficult for the posse to approach unseen.

Firmly Stark banished such concerns from his thoughts. He and Bat had talked them over only moments ago before he'd climbed into the ring. They were Masterson's worries now.

The gambler sat a bit apart from the rest of the audience, closer to the gunman called Dorn. The other Eastern gun, Lecker, was lurking outside the ring. Unlike their Western counterparts, this pair seemed to be taking their watchdogging jobs seriously.

Coolly Stark appraised his opponent. Boullard had the kind of supple, well-muscled build he'd expect with an expert in savate. The bigger man's muscles were those of a good cutting horse, powerful but limber and flexible. They provided the kind of strength and agility needed for this grueling form of combat.

Shrouded in mystery, the beginnings of savate could be traced to seventeenth-century French sailors. Later, the thugs of Paris had learned to favor their feet rather than their fists for brawling. Michael Casseuse had been the first to develop their techniques into an organized fighting system.

He had passed it on to Charles Lecour, who had studied English pugilism and wedded fisticuffs to the brutal French kicks. His student, Charlemont, had toured Europe, challenging all comers: boxers, wrestlers, and brawlers. He had never been defeated. Heavyweight boxing champ John L. Sullivan himself had once been felled by the kicks of a savate fighter.

And Jason Boullard had been trained by Charlemont's top student. The fist and boot champion, Stark reckoned, just might be the most dangerous man he'd ever faced, armed or unarmed.

There was no bell. Standard himself rose and chopped his arm down for it to begin.

Boullard ran at Stark. He was halfway across the ring in two long strides. It was the setup for a high-flying kick to the head, Stark recognized. But right off the mark Boullard fooled him. He went airborne, his body leveling out, one extended leg driving at his target: not Stark's skull, but his kneecap. Boullard's hurtling form seemed to almost skim the ring's floor.

Stark sidestepped him, barely in time, wheeling on the balls of his feet. Boullard caught himself lightly on both hands and one foot, pivoting about to swing his other stiffened leg like a scythe at

Stark's ankles. Again Stark had to dodge clear, and
Boullard catapulted up onto his feet before there
was a chance to counterattack. The spoiler was fast
as blazes.

Boullard came in with fists up. Stark threw a sideward kick at his lead leg to slow him down. Deftly
Boullard turned his calf to absorb the kick, and
whipped his other leg up and around in snapping
arc that drove at Stark's temple. Stark's rigid fore-
arm met his shin. Stark wavered beneath the power
of the blocked kick. He moved in punching with
both hands, low then high. His knuckles bounced
off elbows and forearms, and Boullard hooked a
vicious knee up at him. Stark fouled it with a fore-
arm.

Then, fist and boot, they duelled, both of them
fast as blazes. Their hands blurred in and out like
striking snakes—every bit as deadly. No single
punch was discernible, but somehow there were
arms and shoulders and even other fists to block or
parry most of them. Booted feet landed jarringly
against legs or arms or bodies. They hurt even when
they were deflected, numbing flesh and muscles
with their power.

Somewhere in that flurry of give and take Stark
realized he was getting the worst of it. Here in the
center of the ring. Boullard's height and reach gave
him the advantage. A hooking right corkscrewed his
head around on his neck. He tried a counter but

glimpsed a kick descending like an executioner's ax. He jerked his head out of its path, and the sidewards thrust of his own foot fell short of Boullard's anchor leg, a half heartbeat before the heel of Boullard's foot crashed down onto his shoulder with the impact of a falling log.

He felt his knees buckle as pain tore through his shoulder socket. If he hadn't been twisting to throw the failed kick, he knew his shoulder would've been smashed as surely as Burt's had been by his own .45 bullet. Boullard's followup push kick drove the sole of his boot square into Stark's chest like the end of a railroad tie. Stark went flailing back onto the ropes, his breath gone, his heart almost shocked into stopping permanently.

Possessed, his handsome face made ugly by his leering grin, Boullard tried using the same kick again. The old scars stood out lividly on his features.

Desperately Stark twisted. He felt Boullard's driving boot scrape roughly past his side. Then the bigger man's leg had thrust all the way through the ropes and tangled there. Fire surged in Stark's blood, searing away the pain. With Boullard in the ropes, now the edge was his.

He hooked his fists, one-two, against the hard muscles sheathing Boullard's rib cage, and brought an overhand right down to pound his ear. Boullard surged backward, clearing his leg from its entanglement. Stark started in on him, then checked as Boullard got his guard up and moved to meet him. Stark wasn't about to try to kick or punch it out with the spoiler a second time. He retreated, circling, flicking out front snap kicks to the leg and body, using them like jabs to hold Boullard at bay and try to find his own range.

But with the big man pressing in, lashing out with fists and feet, there was no time for Stark to set himself. He'd have to give himself time. Choosing his moment, he sprang forward at an angle, the thrust of his legs carrying him clear of Boullard's forward rush. From the side he went at his foe, landing a snapping kick and a reaching right before Boullard could wheel and meet his onslaught. The spoiler faded back—right into the ropes as Stark had planned.

He brushed aside the kick Boullard thrust to meet him, and banged with both fists as he made it into range. Covering, Boullard got his forearms up and his elbows together. Stark ripped through them with an uppercut that rocked Boullard's head on his thick neck.

Driving his arms out straight with a convulsive thrust, Boullard shoved him back. The blunt toe of Boullard's right boot swept around and drove in under his rib cage. Pivoting like a dancer, picking up momentum and power with the move, Boullard scythed a high-spinning heel kick that for a piece of a second made Stark's vision go black.

Blindly Stark shot out a side kick that met Boullard's oncoming bulk with a solid jolt traveling back up Stark's leg. He whirled away before Boullard could reach him again. Where had his guard been when that heel kick had come down on him? he wondered numbly. The sequence of the fight was becoming muddled in his mind. Had Boullard landed the last kick, or had he? He knew remotely that neither of them had been knocked down. In a fight of this calibre, if you went down, odds were you wouldn't be getting up again. Ever.

He shook his head to clear his mind. His ears rang like gongs. His side felt as if it had been cut open, and his legs ached as if wrapped in barbed wire. He prayed Boullard was in no better shape. But he had a nasty hunch that wasn't the case.

Boullard loomed before him, maybe slowed just a trifle by the last kick he'd run into. Stark crouched and forced his aching legs to thrust him upward, twirling his body in midair. His leg whip-snapped around with his spin. He'd aimed at Boullard's skull. But Boullard ducked and leapt upward himself so Stark's kick cut thin air. Stark's legs flexed to absorb his landing, and there was no way he could avoid the mirror image of his own kick that Boullard lashed at him in midair.

Senses reeling, he staggered back and felt the

ropes take his weight. Dimly he saw Boullard setting himself for another and final kick.

A flurry of gunshots and yells rolled into the training camp from out on the prairie.

Stark had forgotten his mission, forgotten Masterson and Nix and the illicit fight circuit. Everything had ceased to exist except his foe and the conflict between them, and for the barest instant the sounds made no sense. Then over Boullard's shoulder he saw a pack of yelling shooting riders closing on the camp. The hired guns were just now reacting to this attack from their rear.

Evett and his posse had arrived at last.

Boullard froze as the sounds penetrated his senses. For a single pulsebeat he fought the natural instinct to wheel toward a new danger. In that brief moment Stark found new strength to come off the ropes, spinning in a full tight circle. His right leg lifted high, hooking as he completed the turn, to hammer the heel of his boot square against the base of Boullard's skull.

Like he'd been struck by a sledge at full swing Boullard lurched forward and plunged headfirst over the ropes to the hard ground eight feet below.

A flood of impressions hit Stark. The posse was surging into the camp. It was being met with wild gunfire from those defenders who had chosen to fight rather than take to their heels. Overturned benches made sorry barricades for a few of them.

Stark saw one gunsel straighten to his feet, clutch his chest, and topple backward. A rider, smoking gun in hand, swung his mount in search of other targets.

Rapid movement among the front ranks of the benches drew Stark's eye. Standard and the rest of the tycoons were on their feet, milling in confusion. Masterson had started toward them, only to be confronted by Dorn. The Eastern gunman's hand darted inside his coat, reappearing in the flicker of an eye with some sort of fancy magazine-fed pistol in his fist. Faster, came a gleam of gold in the sunlight as Masterson's cane slashed down.

Dorn cried out and grabbed at his gun wrist, the fancy pistol falling from his grip. Again Masterson struck, as he had in the old days when he'd ridden herd on some of the roughest towns in the West. The golden head of the walking stick met Dorn's temple and dropped him crumpling atop his fallen gun.

Stark vaulted out of the ring. His feet hit the ground beside Boullard. The fighter's massive form sprawled unmoving.

Gunfire cracked and boomed. Masterson had his custom silverplated Colt in action now, swapping shots with the Yanger brothers and Lecker, the other Eastern gun. Smoke hung in a haze. Burt yelled high and shrill and dropped his clumsily held Colt. He toppled among the benches.

Lecker had his gun—another fancy magazine pistol—out, bringing it to bear on Masterson. Stark yelled and rushed him. Lecker pivoted, his gun swinging toward Stark. Before it could come into line, Stark's rising foot met Lecker's gunarm and thrust it skyward. The pistol windmilled away. Hard on the heels of his kick Stark dropped a crashing overhand right to the juncture of Lecker's neck and shoulder. The impact smashed Lecker to his knees. Stark's upthrust knee to the jaw finished him.

Masterson and Clint Yanger were jockeying for position among the benches. Their guns roared in a furious exchange of lead. Stark's eyes searched frantically for Lecker's magazine pistol.

Some fighter's instinct warned him. He spun just in time to take a jolting roundhouse kick from Boullard—incredibly, back on his feet and back in the fight.

Stark's legs tangled with one of the benches and he went over backwards. Boullard towered over him, pile-driving foot upraised to stomp. Stark kicked the fallen bench against his anchor leg and scrambled to his feet as Boullard caught his balance.

Round two, Stark thought grimly. How many times did he have to whip this crazed mauler?

The sole of Boullard's boot drove at him in another battering ram kick. Stark sidestepped and wrapped his arm around the outstretched leg as it thrust past him. Clamping it against his side, he lunged, tilting the bigger man back on his heels. Three times while he held Boullard off balance; three times in not much over a second, Stark sledged his right fist to that point on the jaw boxers called the button.

Cleanly landed, any one of the blows would've done the job, even at the beginning of the fight. Boullard's eyes rolled up in his livid face, and he sagged as if all his bones and muscles had turned to string. Stark lifted his arm to free Boullard's leg and let him fall.

Knockout.

"Don't shoot! I give up!" Clint Yanger flung his six-shooter aside and raised his hands before Masterson's smoking revolver.

Stricken at the turn of events, the huddled trio of Eastern tycoons shakily followed suit.

The rest of the dustup was pretty much winding down. The mounted deputies were corraling the last of the Yanger gun crew. The marshal himself, astride a spirited roan, spurred up and reined his mount to a halt. A revolver was in his fist. For these arrests Nix had left the administration work to someone else.

Another horse pulled up. Thomas grinned down from the saddle. The swarthy fighter looked Stark over. "Whoo-ee, I'm mighty sorry I missed this fight!"

Stark looked askance at him. "Next time you can take my place."

Thomas just grinned the wider.

"Arrived as soon as we could," Nix advised. "Thomas figured you'd be here when we didn't strike pay dirt at the homeplace."

He broke off at the pound of hooves going at a breakneck pace. Decked out fetchingly in riding regalia, Prudence McKay was off her horse in a flash. She darted toward Stark, pausing at the final instant. Even with the dust of the trail on her, Stark reckoned she'd never looked more lovely.

Her trembling hand reached out to touch his bare chest once again. Stark extended a long arm and hugged her to him. He felt the soft brush of her hair against his flesh.

Then she stiffened and he released her.

"Why in the world did you go through with this fight when you knew we were on our way?" she demanded.

"What kind of a fool thing are you doing riding with this posse?" he countered, and cast an accusing glare at Nix over her shoulder.

The lawman shrugged. "Next time *you* try telling her she can't come."

Chapter Fifteen

"You won't be able to get away with this, Miss McKay," Standard blustered in Clint Yanger's office.

Prudence had appropriated the desk for the meeting after first cleaning the mess off of it. Stark had leaned his shoulders against the wall and crossed his arms. He was prepared to watch the goings-on with some satisfaction. Seated in an easy chair, Masterson also looked on with interest.

Busy with handling the pack of gunsels his posse had taken into custody, Marshal Nix had asked Prudence to meet with the Eastern tycoon. Standard had been demanding an explanation for his arrest, and smoking up the air with his profanity. Prudence was

179

more than willing to confront him and lay down the law.

"On the contrary, Mr. Standard," she retorted now. "*You* are the one who is no longer going to get away with conducting illegal prizefights that have resulted in more than one death. You're an accessory to murder, Mr. Standard."

"That's ridiculous, you little—"

"Watch it, pal," Stark interjected.

Standard glared at him but stifled whatever language he'd been about to use in describing Prudence. Oddly, Prudence didn't admonish Stark for his interruption. She seemed almost pleased.

"I've got powerful friends, Miss McKay," Standard tried again.

"Like the two who are under arrest along with you?" Prudence inquired demurely.

"This is outrageous. No one in this forsaken wilderness has any authority to take us into custody and level these types of frivolous charges. As soon as we get to a real court, I'll have the charges dropped, and see you disbarred. Where I come from I *own* the judges and the juries!"

"You're not in New York, Mr. Standard," Prudence reminded. "You're in Indian Territory, subject to Federal law in cases such as this, enforceable by Marshal Nix and the Federal Court system. How many Federal judges do you own out here in this *forsaken wilderness?*"

"I don't care where we are, you won't be able to make these charges stick!"

"I wouldn't lay odds on it, Mr. Standard. In fact, if I was given to wagering, I would wager that your two business associates and co-conspirators, as well as your bodyguards, would be willing to cooperate with the Federal prosecutors to see to it that you bear the brunt of the responsibility, and suffer the consequences."

"They use a noose out here in the wilderness," Stark couldn't resist adding, and this time Prudence did shoot him a sharp glance.

Standard glowered angrily for a moment then stalked back to the deputy acting as his guard. Handcuffed, he was ushered none too gently out of the office.

"Nice work, counselor," Masterson said as he rose easily to his feet. He was his usual dapper self. "Now I have some matters to tend to, if you'll pardon me."

He strode to the door then turned back to eye the two of them with a whimsical quirk to his mouth.

At last his gaze settled on Stark. "You have fine legal representation, Jim. If I was you, I'd put her on a permanent retainer." He gave Prudence what for all the world looked like a wink, tipped his derby, and went out the door before Stark could speak.

Prudence looked a bit flustered, Stark noted with some puzzlement.

"Excuse me, folks." A grinning Thomas appeared in the doorway. "Were you two wanting to be alone?"

"No," Stark and Prudence said at the same moment.

Thomas nodded. "I understand," he assured them, "and I'll just take a moment."

Stark glanced at Prudence. She was blushing to beat all now. His own face felt hot, but that was only his imagination.

"I wanted to congratulate the new champion of fist and boot." Thomas advanced to wring Stark's hand.

"The *last* champion," Prudence said with emphasis.

"Amen to that, Miss Prudence!"

"You're wearing something new." Stark nodded at the U.S. Deputy Marshal's star Thomas had pinned to his shirt.

"This?" Thomas fingered the badge. He was clearly proud of it. "Marshal Nix decided I needed to be a deputy to ride with the posse."

"Looks good there. You figure to make it permanent?"

"I just might. The Marshal has told me he'd welcome me to the ranks. Way I see it, I've been and done a lot of things back down the trail, but I've never been a lawman. Might be fun to try. I'll give my gal a holler to come up this way and join me. We can get some land here and settle down."

"She'll like it here, Thomas," Prudence told him. "The Territories need people like the two of you."

"Why, thank you, Miss Prudence. Now I'll be getting along." He was grinning again for some reason as he departed.

Prudence swung around in her swivel chair to examine Stark in his posistion he'd resumed against the wall. She'd found time to freshen up after the hard ride she'd made with the posse, and one of the feminine guests of Clint and Burt must've provided her with the blouse and skirt she wore. She was an eyeful.

Stark resisted the impulse to go to her. What would he do when he reached her? She didn't get up, and for a heartbeat her pretty face had an expression that could've been hope or fear. He couldn't tell which.

Maybe both.

"Well," she said archly, "are you ready to announce your retirement from the ring?"

Stark cocked his head thoughtfully. " 'Champion of Fist and Boot,' " he mused aloud. "Retiring undefeated. I like the sound of that."

"You'd better," she warned.

"Of course there's still the regular prizefight circuit. Now that I'm sure I ain't lost my punch, I might just try a few bouts."

"Not with me you around, you won't!"

"I was looking for you to be in the front row cheering me on."

"That's not likely. Besides, as I recall, you still owe me dinner and a play and dancing."

"I reckon I do," Stark drawled. "With no arguments, fights or disagreements. Right?"

There was an imp of mischief dancing in Prudence's dark eyes. She raised her dainty fists and squared off in a mock fighting stance. "Just keep your guard up, Champ," she advised.